WELCOME HOME, MRS. JORDON

Books by Janet Lambert

PENNY PARRISH STORIES
Star Spangled Summer 1941
Dreams of Glory 1942
Glory Be! 1943
Up Goes the Curtain 1946
Practically Perfect 1947
The Reluctant Heart 1950

TIPPY PARRISH STORIES
Miss Tippy 1948
Little Miss Atlas 1949
Miss America 1951
Don't Cry Little Girl 1952
Rainbow After Rain 1953
Welcome Home, Mrs. Jordan 1953
Song in Their Hearts 1956
Here's Marny 1969

JORDAN STORIES
Just Jenifer 1945
Friday's Child 1947
Confusion by Cupid 1950
A Dream for Susan 1954
Love Taps Gently 1955
Myself & I 1957
The Stars Hang High 1960
Wedding Bells 1961
A Bright Tomorrow 1965

PARRI MACDONALD STORIES
Introducing Parri 1962
That's My Girl 1964
Stagestruck Parri 1966
My Davy 1968

CANDY KANE STORIES
Candy Kane 1943
Whoa, Matilda 1944
One for the Money 1946

DRIA MEREDITH STORIES
Star Dream 1951
Summer for Seven 1952
High Hurdles 1955

CAMPBELL STORIES
The Precious Days 1957
For Each Other 1959
Forever and Ever 1961
Five's a Crowd 1963
First of All 1966
The Odd Ones 1969

SUGAR BRADLEY STORIES
Sweet as Sugar 1967
Hi, Neighbor 1968

CHRISTIE DRAYTON STORIES
Where the Heart Is 1948
Treasure Trouble 1949

PATTY AND GINGER STORIES
We're Going Steady 1958
Boy Wanted 1959
Spring Fever 1960
Summer Madness 1962
Extra Special 1963
On Her Own 1964

CINDA HOLLISTER STORIES
Cinda 1954
Fly Away Cinda 1956
Big Deal 1958
Triple Trouble 1965
Love to Spare 1967

Dear Readers:

Mother always said she wanted her books to be good enough to be found in someone's attic!

After all of these years, I find her stories—not in attics at all—but prominent in fans' bookcases just as mine are. It is so heart-warming to know that through these republications she will go on telling good stories and being there for her "girls," some of whom find no other place to turn.

With a heart full of love and pride–
Janet Lambert's daughter,
   Jeanne Ann Vanderhoef

WELCOME HOME, MRS. JORDON

BY

Janet Lambert

❦

Image Cascade Publishing
www.ImageCascade.com

MANUFACTURED IN THE UNITED STATES
OF AMERICA

A hardcover edition of this book was originally published by E. P. Dutton & Co. It is here reprinted by arrangement with Mrs. Jeanne Ann Vanderhoef.

First *Image Cascade Publishing* edition published 2000.
Copyright renewed © 1981 by Jeanne Ann Vanderhoef

Library of Congress Cataloging in Publication Data
Lambert, Janet 1895-1973
    Welcome home, Mrs. Jordan.

(Juvenile Girls)
Reprint. Originally published: New York: E. P. Dutton, 1953.

ISBN 978-1-930009-23-3

For

MY NEW GIRLS

(The ones who have just grown up to my books)

Brant Beach, New Jersey
May 2, 1953

My very dear girls:

It has been two years and several books
since I've written you a letter. I do think of you so constantly and enjoy your letters to me, but I never seem to
have time enough for personal chats with you.

Time has passed so quickly since we came to
Brant Beach to live. The faithful Peppi still lies beside my
typewriter while I write about Tippy and Dria, and all the
girls I like so much. I fish from my boat in summer; and,
since we have made this our permanent home, I watch the ocean
roll up to my dunes in winter.

I do hope you will like this last book in
the series about Tippy, and will feel as satisfied and happy
about her future as I do. We can relax now and know she is
going to have a wonderful life with a wonderful husband. Tippy
is one of my favorite girls—and from your letters I know she's
yours, too. Perhaps we'll hear more about her sometime. Through
Susan Jordan? We might.

Poor little Susan began to interest me when she
turned up at Tippy's wedding. I hadn't thought of her for a long,
long time; and even when the smaller Jordons were tearing around,
I didn't notice her much, did you? Now I'm beginning to wonder
what she's really like. Perhaps I'll try to find out.

Thank you, girls, for liking my books. Don't
lose the art of reading, even with television offering such
fascinating entertainment. Read all you can. Read everybody's
books and store away the knowledge; for beautifully assembled
words make paintings in your minds that will never leave you,
and they tell stories you will remember for years to come.

Good-by for now. I love you each and every one.

WELCOME HOME, MRS. JORDON

CHAPTER 1

T IPPY P ARRISH pushed open the front door and bumped through with two clumsy boxes. A large square hatbox hung from one hand and an equally large but longer and bulkier dress box from the other.

"Is anybody home?" she called, closing the door by backing into it.

"Not a soul," came a voice from the living room; and she clung to her purchases as she went on to the wide archway and surveyed a recumbent figure on the divan.

"Well, for goodness' sake, Pen!" she said, surprised. "I didn't expect to see you. What brings you over on such a blustery afternoon? And why aren't you at home with your young? Or in town?"

"One question at a time," Penny Parrish MacDonald answered, laying her magazine on her stomach and an apple core on the coffee table beside her. "I came over to see Mums, who's out, and my young are with me, down by the brook somewhere, and it isn't a blustery afternoon, it's a clear, windy November day. As for being in New York, this isn't a matinee day, so I can have a leisurely dinner at home and drive in to entertain my public whenever Josh says it's time to start. You look quite cute. What did you buy?"

Penny sat up and swung her feet to the floor. She blew an escaping strand of hair out of her eyes, then pulled off a black velvet ribbon and let a whole bronze mass cascade about her shoulders. The magazine slid off to the floor as she waved the ribbon at Tippy's boxes. "More new trousseau?" she asked.

"Lots more." Tippy plumped her boxes on the coffee table and went over to throw the apple core into a lazily burning fire that received it with sputtering pleasure. "Buying clothes is all I have to do," she said plaintively. "It makes me *feel* as if I'm going to be married, at least. Sometimes," she sighed, turning around and knotting her fists into the pockets of her bright red coat, "I wonder if I ever am. I never get any nearer to the day."

"Oh, but you do, pet."

Penny looked at the tense little figure before her and thought how pretty Tippy looked in her gay red outfit. Vivid, which seemed strange, for Tippy Parrish gave the impression of being a fragile girl. Her skin was flawless, her big eyes such a clear, rich hazel, and her short curls made a golden halo above her small face.

"You should buy a red coat," Penny said suddenly, "and stop borrowing mine. Red's good on you."

"But better on you." Tippy slid out of the coat and tossed it on a chair. "You're the sparkling one," she said without envy, "the rich and dazzling actress of the family. Red's really for you, and royal purple and ermine."

"Why, I do thank you." Penny retied her ribbon, knotting the curls into a spray on her neck, and she said with her brown eyes laughing, "Now that we have discussed the weather and exchanged compliments, how about showing me your loot?"

"All right—but I'm not sure I like some of it much." Tippy started to slide heavy twine over the end of the dress box, then stopped. "Honestly, Pen," she said glumly, "I'm in a most discouraging situation. I hunt clothes and I hunt clothes, but my bridegroom never shows up. At first I bought early fall dresses, then I had to take most of those back and exchange them for winter things. By the time I get married, if I ever do, it'll be spring and I'll be needing cottons."

"Pooh." Penny really laughed aloud this time, for Tippy looked so young and woeful. "Peter's only stationed in Texas," she pointed out. "He can't up and leave until he gets his orders. You're an army brat, so you should know the army always functions in a peculiar manner. My goodness," she said, "I can remember the times when we Parrishes used to pack up and be ready to move, then wait and wait. Or else the orders came when we weren't expecting them so soon, if at all. And there was the time we went all the way to San Francisco and found we had to go back to Ethan Allen in Vermont."

"I don't remember that."

"You weren't even born."

Penny abandoned her interest in the contents of the boxes and decided to strengthen Tippy's waning morale. "Mums and Dad just had three of us," she said, enjoying the memory, "and we were headed for Honolulu. David was grumpy because he had had to leave his pet alligator behind and I was sure I'd never find another friend as nice as a little girl I'd just met in first grade. She had yellow pigtails and I kept wanting Mums to braid my curls. Bobby just wanted his bottle. He wouldn't drink his milk out of a cup, and he splashed it all over the dining car and all over us. Mums and Dad were the only happy ones. I guess they were so glad to be taking us somewhere that was warm, where they wouldn't have to bundle us up in coats and galoshes and listen to us sniffle and cough all winter, that they didn't care how hard the trip was. Well," she ended, "the orders had been changed by the time we got to San Francisco, and nothing went to Honolulu but the grand piano."

"Why did it go?" Tippy asked.

"Because they couldn't find it in the hold of the transport. All the rest of our furniture was taken off and stacked in its crates on the dock, but the piano had been put in with someone else's stuff and it was time for the transport to sail—so away it went. It took almost a year for us to get it back."

"I'm glad we finally did."

Tippy looked at the piano before the windows at the end of the long room, and especially at a group of photographs in silver frames on its polished mahogany. David's wedding picture was there with Carrol's, who was so beautiful she took one's breath away, and their two little sons on their ponies; Penny, laughing and looking about to hop out of her frame, was beside dark, craggy Josh who adored her, and little Parri and Joshu, cute but obviously posed by a photographer. And of course there was Bobby, stiff and handsome above the high collar of his West Point uniform, and looking as if he were truly kind and loveable. Wrinkling her nose at Bobby, she said, "Well, I'm glad we didn't lose it, but I do wish Mums and Dad would let us put their pictures on it."

"They won't." Penny was still interested in the contents of the boxes; so, to draw Tippy out of her restrospection she suggested, "Look above the family heads and see if my two blessings are still alive."

"There's a red snow suit out there and a smaller blue one," Tippy reported. "The red one's sitting on the blue one."

"Joshu can take care of himself. Now come back here," she invited, patting a cushion beside her, "and tell me just why you're in such a hurry to have Peter come back so you can go off and leave us."

"I want to be married, you dope." Tippy turned away from the window and asked bluntly, "Didn't you?"

"Naturally. But I was marrying Josh. And I didn't have to go way off to Germany or give up my career."

"*My* career was a lovely thing." Tippy rolled her eyes upward as she remembered the few long months she had spent running errands in a television studio. "I hope no one ever so much as mentions it to me again. Why," she said, coming back to stand before the divan, "I feel hot and sticky every time I think about last summer. Being an apprentice in business is very different from being a famous actress," she pointed out.

"Everyone has to start at the bottom," Penny retorted, "I did. And if Peter Jordon were a general instead of a first lieutenant, he could have quite a bit to say about his own future plans, instead of waiting for someone to decide to transfer him to Germany. He has to learn patience."

"I know it." Tippy untied the brown tape on the hatbox, then stopped again without lifting the lid. "I don't mean to be fussy," she said, "but you'll have to admit it's been a long wait. The wonderful Mr. Jordon flies in, late in August, and sweeps me off my feet. And he stays two weeks. And he says, 'I'll be right back and headed for Europe, so be ready to go with me.' And Mums telephones all our friends, alerting them for a wedding—because we won't have time to send out invitations—and and all we do is wait. And postpone. And wait. People who were invited to a garden wedding are now taking their fur coats out of storage. They've held out so many Saturdays in their engagement books that whenever Mums calls them now, they sort of hesitate and say, 'Marje, don't you think we should make it just a tentative date?'"

Penny laughed and said with apparent pride, "*That's* the army for you."

"And the Officers Club on Governors Island—where we finally decided to have the reception, when it got too cold to stay outdoors—seems to forget that the Parrishes and Jordons lived on the Island for a long time. It hems and haws, and finally ends up by hedging, 'Our Saturday nights are very busy, you know. If you could give us a definite date. . . .' A definite date! Fat chance." Even Tippy saw humor in the situation and had to laugh. But she did say ruefully, "If it hadn't taken me so long to discover I was in love with Peter, I'd have had a whole year with him by now, in Texas. I don't see why I was so stupid."

"There was Ken Prescott," Penny said. It seemed she was never to see the hat and dresses, so she snatched the opportunity to ask, "You don't grieve for Ken now, do you, cherub?"

"No." Tippy's little face was serene as she answered, "I loved him very much, I'll always love him. Peter understands that. The world stopped for a while, when word came that he'd been killed in Korea. I hurt so terribly in my heart—I still hurt sometimes, but not when I'm with Peter." Tippy stopped and clasped her hands together. "No one has ever been so wonderful as Peter. Not even Ken. Not even Dad, Penny, who's almost perfect. There isn't anyone as fine and wonderful as he is. I can't understand why I didn't discover it sooner, when he was right here in West Point and I lived so close to him, or even when we all lived on Governors Island and I saw him all the time. Why, he's perfect!"

"We know it, pet. We all feel that way about the men we love."

Penny had often wondered, during the months of Tippy's engagement to Peter Jordon, if she truly loved him or had simply taken his love on the rebound, as a release from loneliness and a second best thing. She had been afraid to ask. But now, looking at the distraught maiden across the coffee table, she could say lightly, because of her own happy marriage and ten years' difference in their ages, "You're making a good choice, Tip. You stick it out and Peter will show up one of these days. We'll all clap on our hats and dash for the church."

"I'll pass you on the way."

Tippy finally laid back tissue paper and lifted out a black felt something that looked very small to have needed such a large nest. "I thought it might be rather nice for traveling," she said, perching the creation on her finger. "When I board the ship, if I ever do."

"Put it on."

Tippy sailed her red cap onto the chair with her coat and stood on tiptoe to look into the high mirror above the mantel. "I think it should go farther back and more to one side," she said, turning around.

There was very little hat to be seen. Whoever had designed it had thoughtfully kept it from interfering with a pretty face; and Penny said, "It's all right. It's the kind that, seen from the rear, makes you wonder what sort of girl is under it in front, if you get what I mean. It's a hat you should walk backwards in."

"Then I'll return it." Tippy snatched off the bit of felt and dropped it carelessly into its box, but Penny shook her head.

"No, don't," she said. "It's smart. What else have you?"

"A suit. But I think it's too lightweight for this time of year. Every time I buy anything I try to imagine how it will look on me in Paris, or if it will do to travel around Italy in. I keep forgetting that we'll be living in Germany, with very little money to spend on travel. It won't be like the year I was stationed over there with Mums and Dad, and we took trips. Lieutenants don't dash off to Switzerland or the Riviera. I have a lot of ski clothes left over from then," she explained, pulling out a woolly green jacket and a pair of matching pants, "but I wore them when—when Ken came down from Munich and we skied. I wore them when he joined us that Christmas in Switzerland, too. I thought it might make Peter happier if I have new ones. Do you think so?"

Her amber eyes were wide and troubled as she held the bulky green coat before her, and Penny nodded. "I do, Tip. Start out all new."

"That's what I thought, so I bought the suit. I'll buy new sweaters, too, and new skis, I think. My old ones have a nick that Ken sanded down and mended."

Because she would be living in Germany again, Ken figured in every plan Tippy made, in everything she bought. Europe would be filled with memories of good-looking, winsome Kenneth Prescott, and he would be with Tippy and Peter even on their honeymoon, for he had sailed on the same transport with her before. She had been sixteen then, impressionable and lonely; and Penny grumbled silently to herself, "I wish the children could live somewhere else. They'll have one strike against them at the very start of their marriage." Then she looked up to hear Tippy saying happily:

"I'll have so much to show Peter. It won't be as dull as it was before, with only Ken to come down and cheer me up now and then, and Mums really running the house. And," she continued, grinning, "I won't have lessons to do, this time. I'll be twenty years old, and married. Won't it be fun?"

"Yes, I really think it will be." Penny stood up, took a black taffeta dress out of the box and shook it. "The store certainly smashed things in," she said, sending tissue paper flying. "I like this. I'd like to stay and see you model it, but it's getting late. Perhaps I can come tomorrow—no, it's Wednesday, and I have a matinee. Thursday, I'll see it."

"Pen." Tippy waded through the tissue paper to put her arms around Penny's waist. "You're so good to me," she said lovingly. "I couldn't buy half of these beautiful clothes with the little dab I saved up from my job. And Dad's retired pay, even with the money he makes from his radio news broadcasts, doesn't stretch far enough. I really didn't intend to, but I am spending some of that fabulous check you gave me."

"You should. That's what it's for, that and having some money of your own after you're married. I think David's planning a little donation, too. You see, cherub," she said, tilting up Tippy's chin, "we both know the army. It's a wonderful life, but you'll never be rich."

"I know it, too. Oh, Pen, I do love you."

Hazel eyes and brown smiled at each other before Penny dropped a light kiss on Tippy's cheek and walked over to tap on the windowpane. "It's time for a working gal to be on her way," she said. "When Mums comes home, tell her that I'll be over day after tomorrow and that I have two tickets put away for those friends of hers. Joshu? Parri?" she mouthed, knowing the children couldn't hear her but would see her moving lips and beckoning finger. "Come on. Hurry."

Tippy was picking up her tissue paper, and she stopped crushing it into the box to turn and ask, "Are you planning to stay on in the play this summer?"

"Ask Josh. He's my producer," Penny answered, hunching her shoulders. "I'm only the acting half of the team." Then her eyes twinkled and she said, in a way that was supposed to be offhand and casual, "He goes around mumbling about our being due for a vacation. He says a trip to Europe. . . ."

"Oh, Pen, *would* you? *Would* you come to visit us?" Tippy left the box lid half on to whirl and clasp her hands in supplication.

"We might."

"With Peter and me, in our own house? Pen, will you promise? Could you bring Mums and Dad, too?"

"And David and Carrol, and little Davey and Lang, and the new baby, too, if they have it in time? How about a few Jordons?"

"Everybody," Tippy planned. "We'd have a house party."

"I'm sure it would tickle Peter to death."

Penny's tone was dry, and she scolded, "Stop being a nitwit. You're going off to be with a husband, not entertain a whole family. Remember that, cherub. Just Peter. I think every young couple should be uncluttered by family for at least a year."

"But you're coming, you and Josh."

"Perhaps. For a couple of days, but put it out of your mind and think about your marriage. That's the important thing, right now."

"I can't," Tippy said cheerfully. "I haven't a bridegroom—yet. He won't come and marry me."

The telephone, on a small desk by the back window, set up a shrill clamor; and as she went over to answer it, the hall was filled with high, childish chatter and excited barking.

"Hello?" she said, trying to hear. "Down, Switzy." And she pushed away a small black French poodle that was ecstatically happy to see her again. "Hello? Yes, it is," and she looked back at Penny. "Fort Sam Houston is calling!" she cried, holding out the receiver. "Hang on to this thing till I get upstairs where it's quiet. Oh, it's my bridegroom!"

"Call me tonight, if there's any news." Penny caught the receiver as Tippy dashed past her.

"Oh, golly, golly, I will!"

She swung around the archway toward the stairs and only paused long enough to kiss a pixy that looked exactly like Penny, and give a quick hug to a fat little gnome with two round eyes above a plaid muffler. "Hello and good-by, darlings," she called back, trying not to step on Switzy as he passed her in the race.

She was breathless when she fell across her bed and snatched the black instrument that could bring Peter to her. "Hello, hello," she kept panting, above a bumbling and buzzing in her ear; and she ordered knowingly, "Get off the line, Pen. This is private."

A hasty click answered her, and she rolled over on her back to grin at the ceiling. Then she sat up straight and breathed, "Oh, Peter, darling, where are you?"

"In the hall of my B.O.Q.," a beautiful rumble came back into the room.

"Standing up or sitting down?"

"Sitting in a phone booth, why?"

"I can't see you. Wait a minute." She tumbled off the bed and snatched a photograph from her dressing table. "There," she said, setting it on the little night stand before her. I'm sitting here, looking at you, in my room. Go on."

A deep chuckle meant that Peter was playing the game with her, and he said, "Of course you can see I'm in uniform. What're you wearing?"

"My old green wool that you liked. Oh, darling, you do look so handsome!"

Peter knew her eyes were resting on a photographer's piece

of clever work, and that he wasn't handsome at all. His face was too thin and long, his cheekbones too high. But he did have fine gray eyes under level brows, a wide, intelligent smile, and smooth, neatly parted hair that stayed the color of ripe wheat.

"Oh, I wish I could see the *real* you," Tippy wailed.

"Honey, listen." Hers was the face he wanted to see, not the familiar one that greeted him in the mirror every morning, so he said quickly, "Tip, my overseas orders are changed."

"You can't come back!" she cried, without waiting.

"Of course I can, childie, I'm coming."

"But you're going on to Korea." Fear gripped Tippy. She clung to the telephone as two tears squeezed out and onto her lashes. "You're going out to the Far Eastern Command, is that it?"

"No, darling. Wherever I'm going, you're going with me. Can you hear that, Tip? We'll soon be together."

"Oh." She closed her eyes and the two tears slid down and away. "You frightened me," she said in almost a whisper. "I thought I'd missed being married to you."

"You haven't. Not if you want to string along. But my orders have been changed, Tip. Can you hear me? I'm not going to Europe. I'm ordered to Panama."

"Where?"

"To Panama. To the 45th Tank Battalion, at Fort Clayton."

"Oh, shades of Gussie!" The whole collection of winter clothes she had bought paraded across Tippy's mind like a fashion show. She forgot she was to be married, at last, and could think only of the suits, the woolens, and especially of the fur coat she had bought. For Panama—a place that was hotter than the hammers! "My soul," she said.

"How does it strike you?"

"Like a sock in the teeth." And she asked, as if he could help her, "What shall I do about all my clothes?"

"Pack 'em," he answered happily. "I leave here two weeks from tomorrow and we sail on the twenty-second of December."

"But. . . ." Tippy wanted to shout, "I've bought all *winter* clothes and Panama's a very tropical place." She wanted to impress upon him that not only were his plans changed, hers were knocked into a cocked hat. But what would Peter know about all the shopping she would have to do, or coaxing stores to take back dresses she had owned for over two months? "Oh, dear," she gulped; and he asked quickly:

"Don't you want to go there, Tip?"

"I want to go anywhere with you, my goodness, yes," she rallied quickly. "I'll go if I haven't anything to take but a faded cotton dress and my last year's bathing suit. When—when did you say we sail?"

"On the twenty-second of December. O.K. with you, darling?"

"Oh, very O.K. And you'll really be here just two weeks from the day after tomorrow! I can't believe it. Oh, Peter, I have so much to do before then, and Mums can actually *invite* people now. It is definite, isn't it?"

"It's set this time, absolutely set." The operator cut in to announce, "Your three minutes are up," but Peter forestalled the disconnection by shouting, "Hey, don't cut us off till I hang up"; and went on as if there had been no interruption, "Are you happy about it?"

"I guess so. I'll tell you more about that when you come. The important thing right now is—we have plans to make."

They talked on and on, with Tippy refusing to look at the little clock on the table before her as it ticked valiantly and accurately on, and Peter not listening to his wrist watch, so close to his ear.

"That does it," he finally said. "Nothing to do now but wait till I come!"

Nothing to do but wait! Tippy couldn't help the gasp she gave. Why, she had a whole wardrobe to exchange and a wedding to plan! Goodness only knew how she could ever accomplish it all.

"I love you so much," Peter broke into her chaotic thoughts to say. "Good-by, childie, darling."

Childie. What a silly nickname. Sillier even than the cherub Penny had started and Ken had picked up. But so dear, so sweet when Peter said it, for he wasn't given to extravagant endearments. He wrenched out compliments as if he were whacking a nail on the head with a hammer. So Tippy replied softly, "Good-by, most wonderful man in the world," and waited to be sure there would be no further sound of his voice.

CHAPTER 11

TIPPY went flying down the stairway. "I'm going to be married!" she shouted. "At last I'm getting *married*. Here comes the bride—ta-tum-ta-tum. Hoo-ray for Tippy Parrish!"

She swirled into the living room where her mother and father had just met to discuss their day apart, and spun about like a green top gone berserk.

"Well, well, well," Colonel Parrish said, running his hand through his gray hair and watching her with amused blue eyes. "Love seems to have knocked you off your rocker."

He had often watched Penny dance about like that, gay and abandoned in her excitement, but rarely had he seen the quiet Tippy come so joyously alive. Not for a long time. Seldom since she had grown to sudden womanhood by falling in love with Ken, and certainly never since the word of Ken's death in Korea had come. So he laid down the cigarette he had been about to light and held out his arms. "Shall we dance?" he asked.

"With pleasure." Tippy swung him around, then rushed at her mother on the divan. "You can engage the club now," she cried, rumpling her mother's curls that were still almost as brown as Penny's, and patting her firm cheek. "Any old date. Everything's *wonderful!*"

She flung up her arms and would have gone on whirling but Switzy leaped up at her. He wanted to be in the fun, too, so she said, "All right, chum, we'll dance together. Here we go."

Switzy took backward steps and was pulled forward again, emitting yelps. Her grasp hurt his paws, so she kissed him on his fuzzy nose and let him drop. "He'll have to have a haircut," she said suddenly. "It's hot in Panama."

Two pairs of startled eyes widened and two mouths stayed open, their laughter stopped. "Yep, that's where we're going," she panted, and dropped down onto an ottoman to tell them all about it.

"Peter's ordered to Fort Clayton," she said, "to some sort of a tank outfit, and we'll have a house. A whole house of our own. We'll pick bananas and pineapples for breakfast, and I'll perish of heat in the wool dresses I've bought. I'll go around panting, like this," she jumped up to demonstrate.

She made noises that rivaled Switzy's after his dance, and their duet gave her father time to light his cigarette and her mother to run to the desk for her notebook.

"Tippy, calm down," Mrs. Parrish begged, when she was sure she had a real wedding to plan, not another false alarm. "How can we work out anything with all this nonsense going on? Dave, stop goading her into being such an idiot."

"I think she's funny." Colonel Parrish sat down in his favorite chair where he could watch the happy statue in the middle of the floor. "Go on, Tippy, prance some more."

"I'm about pranced out." Tippy sagged to show her fatigue, but Switzy began to bark, shrilly and in excited circles. "Bless me, he's calling Trudy," she cried, and went leaping into the hall. "Oh, Trudy, my love," she shouted, "come in here. I'm leaving. I'm practically on my way to the Canal Zone."

The swinging door between the dining room and a service pantry popped open and a brown face and bit of large white apron showed. "I knows it," Trudy answered, her smile as wide as Tippy's. "I heard the ruckshuns. I'll come in a minute."

"Now!" Tippy commanded. "Let the dinner burn. Let all Rome burn. Countrymen, lend me your ears! Colonel and Mrs. David Craig Parrish request the honor of the whole world's presence at the marriage of their daughter Andrea, to an incredibly wonderful man. Come one, come all—and especially, you come, this minute."

"All right." Trudy gave in with a resigned sigh and advanced warily. "No jumpin' me around like you did your papa," she warned, still in the safety of the dining room. "My dancin' days is over."

"Oh, frail one, I'll be very tender with you." Tippy put the neat little person who had been a faithful and loving mainstay through all her joys and troubles carefully into a chair. "Who's going to bake a chocolate cake for Peter when he comes?" she asked, standing over her.

"Me," Trudy answered obediently.

"Who's going to sit right beside Mums in the church and see that she gets up at just the right minute to join Dad and me at the altar, the way she did at Penny's wedding?"

"Me."

"And who's going to have a heartfelt talk with the bride some evening? To tell her how much being married to the one she loves means, and not to waste time being homesick and lonesome for Mums and Dad and you?"

"I reckon I am," Trudy answered. "Though how you knows so much beats me."

"Penny told me. Besides, you're always giving us good advice." Tippy winked, then stood up straight and spread out her arms. "Start planning!" she commanded.

"I don't know how to go about it." Mrs. Parrish riffled the pages of her notebook, then looked up to say wryly, "I've done everything and canceled it all so many times the pages are a mess. I can't even read my guest list. If anyone can make any sense out of this. . . ."

She held out the scribbled notes with pretended inadequacy. Something was squeezing her heart. This was final. This was the real wedding, she knew it was; and no amount of working toward it had quite prepared her for this moment. Tippy was really going away. Dear little Tippy who brought in the very sun, was taking it out.

"Seems like," Trudy said, knowing, "seems like we ought to collect ourselves and go at this thing with our stomachs happy. We don't have to work it all out in one minute."

"Yes, we do. We have to hurry."

Tippy was adamant and blindly pushing time along, but her father crushed out his cigarette in an ash tray and said carefully, not to reveal his own sadness, "Let's take Trudy's advice. Mums and I will help her tonight, and you'll have time to do a little telephoning around. Penny should be told the news, she may not have left for the theater, yet, and there are David and Carrol to notify, and Bobby."

"And Alcie. Alcie's going to be my maid of honor, so she should be among the first to know the exact date of her brother's wedding." Tippy stopped and looked at her mother. "When is the exact date?" she asked.

"We'll have to decide." Mrs. Parrish took a calendar from the back of her notebook and bent her head to study it. Sudden tears clouded her eyes and blurred the figures, so that she listened gratefully to her husband urge:

"Later, Marge. Everything depends on the transport sailing date . . ."

"That's the twenty-second," Tippy cut in.

". . . and Peter's plans for a honeymoon."

"My soul, I forgot to ask him about that." Tippy clapped a hand over her mouth and was about to dash upstairs to the telephone again when she suddenly remembered something else. "I forgot to ask him where I can reach him this evening, too. Now we are in a picklement."

"Then, suppose we take it easy and discuss some of the things *we* have to handle," he suggested mildly.

"And I'll call up everybody I know. Mercury straps his wings on his heels and is off!"

Tippy went bounding up the stairs again, by-passing Switzy, as usual. She was almost too excited to dial numbers, but she began to calm down when she was told that Penny and Josh had already left for their drive into New York, Carrol and David had gone to a dinner party, and Bobby had marched off to the mess hall. That left only Peter's half-sister, Alice. Alice lived down in Pennsylvania, almost to Philadelphia, and she was sure to be at home and cooking dinner for her own new husband, so Tippy gave the familiar number of the young Draytons and settled back to wait.

The conversation was apt to be long. Alice, after all, was partly responsible for the coming event. She, so Tippy constantly and happily informed her, had given a small week end house party with cataclysmic and carefully planned results. She had been a matchmaker. She had brought competition into her rural setting that was so peaceful it might have been dull, in the form of a pretty sister-in-law. Oh, she had been very sly and scheming.

Tippy tapped the telephone while she waited and enjoyed

a few memories. Her mind flashed far back to the time on Governors Island when she and Alice had solemnly sworn to marry each other's brothers. Fickle Alice. She hadn't fulfilled her part of the bargain, Tippy thought pleasantly, stuffing pillows behind her so she could comfortably remind her of that. Her name was Drayton now, not Parrish, and Bobby was still a lonely cadet. It amused Tippy to think of the harum-scarum Bobby as being lonely for anyone, and it was some time before she realized that her telephone was ringing uselessly.

Alice, too, was out. The one long ring and a short went on until she banged the receiver down and told Switzy, "It isn't fair. Here I am with astounding news to pass on, and not a soul stays home to hear it. The best I can do is repeat it to you."

The telling lasted all of five minutes. Switzy was bored to hear that he was moving South, to a very hot country. He was to have all his warm woolly curls cut off and would wear a new red sweater until he was in a kennel on a ship. He, so she told him, was in a much better position than she was, because electric clippers could remove his fur coat and the one she owned was a financial problem that might stick to her.

He panted uncomfortably while she talked to him, not from the graphic pictures of heat she painted, but because he was too close to a radiator, so she gave up in disgust.

"Oh, come on," she said at last, offering him reluctant release. "You're no help, so I might as well go back downstairs."

The dining-room table was partly set. Her mother was finishing it in an absent-minded way, and Tippy took the flat silver from her. "Scoot," she said. "I'm used to this."

Trudy tired easily now. Her gnarled hands were as deft as ever, but she suffered from arthritis, so the Parrishes gave her all the help she would accept. Tippy laid down knives and forks as if she were slapping railroad ties into place and ran an eager train of plans across them.

"I'll do something about that useless fur coat first thing in the morning," she said. "Thank goodness, it hasn't been sent out yet, but I'll bet my name's already been embroidered in the lining. I bought it a week ago. I'll have to return a slipper satin formal, too, and the velveteen and the . . . oh, dear. To say nothing of tweed skirts, plaid skirts, the wool jumper dress, the jersey, the tan wool and the gray one. I suppose I'll have to keep the two taffetas, I've had them the longest. Never was a bride so utterly wrong!"

"We'll work it out, darling. Penny will go in and help you." Mrs. Parrish had her own problems, and she leaned against the buffet while Tippy worked. "Let me see," she considered, "if you could be married just a day or two before you sail, I think Mr. Thomas would rush the invitations for me and we'd still have time to send them out."

"Don't worry about it. We'll have a wedding. If people don't get there it doesn't matter, because we'll have our families. General Jordon's clear off in Turkey, and his kids are scattered all over creation, so as long as we have Alcie and Jon for Peter, and all of you, I'm satisfied."

"I'd like invitations."

"Hey!" Tippy suddenly said, plopping a silver dish with ivy in it on the center of a lace runner. "Have you ever considered having the wedding in the West Point chapel? We only live about fifteen minutes from there, and we could all come back here and have a nice little party."

"Why, Tippy!" Mrs. Parrish cried, startled out of her complicated planning. "Penny was married in the Governors Island chapel, all the grandchildren have been christened there, and it's much more convenient for our friends. And what would we do with the ones who may have to stay over?"

"What are we going to do with them on Governors Island?" Tippy wanted to know.

"Engage rooms at the Club Annex for them."

"Why not the Thayer Hotel, at West Point? Bobby could come to the wedding then."

"And Penny couldn't." Tippy had started a whole new set of plans, and her mother pointed out patiently, "You're to sail on Monday. If you're married the Saturday night before, as I hope you'll be, Penny can barely make it between her matinee and the evening performance. Even so, we'll have to start the wedding at seven-thirty on the dot, instead of the usual eight o'clock."

"I sound like a schedule," Tippy laughed; and she chanted, "Governors Island special, track one, all aboard."

"And Bobby can be there, too. I think his Christmas leave starts that Friday night."

"Christmas! Oh, Mums, I won't be home for Christmas!"

The wedding was pushed into second place as holly, lighted candles, voices singing carols, and a family around a decorated pine tree crowded in. "How can Peter and I celebrate Christmas out in the middle of an ocean?" she asked.

"Together. Just the way you'll do it in Panama for the next two years."

"We'll postpone going. By cracky, we'll take the January transport." Tippy tossed her head and was about to rearrange the army when she saw the tolerant amusement on her mother's face. "Pack my Christmas gifts in a box," she said flatly. "I'll be married on Governors Island and maybe there'll be a bad storm and the silly old boat won't be able to sail."

"Silly old boats aren't bothered too much by storms," Mrs. Parrish retorted, "especially when they're going into southern waters. Now get on with your work and leave me to mine."

"Bossy!"

The days that followed were hectic. Tippy carried winter dresses to town each morning and came back at night bearing thin ones. Penny's patronage at the furriers was of the sort that sent saleswomen scurrying to the front of the shop whenever she appeared, so the fur coat was relined and restored to its case. Tippy was worn out from saying, "Oh, you're so very kind," to department store managers and tramping about in New York's first sleet storm, looking at cruise clothes and cottons designed for Florida wear.

The invitations were out. Mr. Thomas had bounced about on his fat little legs and promised to do his best for the army. "I must do my bit," was the way he put it, "for Uncle Sam and his fighting men." It was Peter's magic name that sped the engravers but it was Tippy's tongue that licked envelopes until even candy tasted like glue.

"Darned expensive," she muttered, sliding her fist along the flap of the last one, "counting all the telephone calls back and forth to Texas. If I've forgotten a single one of Peter's friends and classmates, may I be strung up and hanged."

"Then take this last batch into town with you and mail them," her mother answered, packing the square white envelopes in a box. "If we have the wedding on a Saturday—it is to be on Saturday, isn't it?"

"I should hope so, since it says so right here." Tippy held up an open invitation and read from it, " 'Saturday, December twentieth.' And here's a reception card for the Governors Island Officers Club, in case you've forgotten there's to *be* a reception following the nuptial event. Have you got it all straight?"

"Oh, I hope so. Really," Mrs. Parrish looked down at the box and shook her head to clear it, "it's all been so hurried and I'm so confused."

"It's about as hurried as a stroll in the park," Tippy laughed, ready to start off on another shopping expedition. "It's all we've talked about for over three months. Just pity me as I plow around in the stores."

And so it went on, day after day, until it was time for Peter to come.

"Expect me when you see me," he had said on his last telephone call from Texas, the morning he started. "Cross-country driving's apt to be slow in winter, you know." But he was making good time, his constant messages confirmed it, and this was the day.

Tippy spent most of the afternoon in the wide bay window. "What are you supposed to wear when your bridegroom comes?" she asked anyone who passed near her. "Something old that he can recognize you in, or part of your third trousseau?"

It didn't matter what answer she received for she changed her dress at regular intervals. And since afternoon twilight had faded to dusk, lamps glowed softly, and a prodded fire worked busily on a new stick of wood before headlights slashed the dark, she was dressed for dinner in a new paper-taffeta print.

"He's here! He's here!" she shouted to her parents who had diplomatically secluded themselves upstairs. And she threw open the front door and flew down the steps.

Ice clung to the brick and Tippy's heels were high. She met Peter at the bottom in a grand skid that almost knocked his breath out. "Whoa," he said, saving them both. "Hang on."

"Forever. Oh, Peter!"

With her arms clamped around his neck, she was warmer out in the cold than she had been inside. The sleeves of his

36

army short-coat were better than a muffler around her, and she could have stayed right there until the wedding.

But Peter kissed her twice, another time for luck, and took half of the muffler away. "In you go," he said, "before you turn into an icicle." And he boosted her up the steps and over the slick place.

Inside the hall, he closed the door and took her in his arms again. "Childie," he said softly against her hair, "we're together now for keeps. Nothing can ever part us again."

"Nothing," she whispered with a happy sigh, resting against him. "I'm just beginning to understand why I was in such a fever of impatience to marry you. I feel relaxed and happy, and —so contented. I feel satisfied with everything, and safe. Do you feel that way, too?"

"I feel like a king. All the way across the continent I sang louder than the radio. Why, every time I had to stop for gas," he said, grinning down at her, "I'd tell the attendant, 'Step on it, Joe. I'm on my way to be married.' I even bought sandwiches and containers of coffee so I could drive while I ate. I hated the hours when I had to knock off to sleep."

"You must be terribly tired."

"Me? I'm as peppy as a jay bird." He lifted her off the floor and swung her around to prove it. "The only time I got tired," he said, "was when I was packing up and clearing the post, and that was just because everyone else was so slow. I could have done it in half the time, alone. My traveling mate got tired though. He slept most of the way."

"Who came with you?" Tippy pulled back to ask. "Another officer? Oh, Peter, you should have made him do part of the driving."

"He couldn't." Peter looked down at her, his gray eyes twinkling. "He doesn't know how. It was Rollo."

"Oh, the poor little dog. Why, I even forgot you had him. Let's bring him in." Tippy squirmed around to reach for the doorknob, but Peter held her.

"He's quite comfortable out there," he said. "He's used to sleeping in cars. I'll take him down to Alcie tomorrow."

"You'll do no such thing." She let go of the knob and pressed his thin cheeks between her hands as she asked, "Do you think it's fair for Switzy to go to Panama, and Rollo have to stay home? He's an army dog. He's always been one, and how do you think he'd feel, stuck off in the country instead of on an army post? I'm ashamed because I didn't remember about Rollo."

But Peter only took her hands away and went on smiling and shaking his head.

"Army folk don't always have it so plush," he said. "Rollo may have had ten years in the army, but he grew up with Alcie and will be quite happy with her."

"Peter Jordon." Tippy managed to plant herself squarely on her two feet and attain a dignified height, which, while not comparable to his six feet, at least put her eyes on a level with his chin. "Rollo," she stated, "is going with us." And she asked, "How would you have felt, when your father married your stepmother, if he had told her, 'You can't bring Alcie and Gwenn to live with us?' How would they have felt?"

"Not too good, I admit. But Rollo's just a dog."

"And I'm his stepmother."

Voices carefully announced the progress of two people along the upstairs hall, and she turned her head to warn, "You might as well go back again. We're having a quarrel."

But Colonel and Mrs. Parrish appeared at the top of the stairway and came on down. "What's she doing to you, son?"

Colonel Parrish asked, holding out his hand as Peter snatched off his cap and sprang up to meet them.

And Mrs. Parrish said, "Oh, Peter, I'm so ashamed of my child," before she kissed him.

"You ought to be ashamed of Peter," Tippy declared, prancing up the steps, too, to crowd in like a substitute player, trying to be in on the signals. "*He's* the one to be ashamed of. Anyone who would leave a little dog out in the cold might not even be kind to me. He might leave me down in Panama."

"Is Rollo with you?" Mrs. Parrish remembered the little gray dog of no particular breed that had trotted around Governors Island, and would have hurried down and outside but Peter held her back.

"He's all right, Mrs. Parrish, really he is," he protested. "I'll bring him in when I unload the car." And he said teasingly to Tippy, "Rollo is a gentleman. I invited him in when I pulled up, but he said politely, 'Oh, run along, old boy and meet your girl. I'm quite cozy out here.' "

"He was always very courteous, even when he upset my garbage can."

Marjory Parrish's dimples winked, and even the smaller dot beside Tippy's mouth twinkled as her lips quirked up in the smile she couldn't hold back. But she did take Peter by both his ears and say with her face close to his. "Rollo's part mine now. He's *going* with us."

"Won't Switzy mind?"

"He'll jolly well like it. He'll have to be just as much a gentleman as Rollo is and just as nice to him as you were to Alcie and Gwenn, or he can find himself new parents."

The greetings on the stairway were over. Colonel and Mrs. Parrish went on down; and Peter said softly, "I love you.

You're just the kind of girl I love," before he and Tippy followed them, and he watched her hang his coat away in the hall closet, fussily, and as if she wanted it to be comfortable there.

"Now," she said, when his service cap had the best place on the shelf, with all the other hats crowded aside, "you can pay your respects to Trudy while I inform Mr. Only Child that he has a new brother."

"He won't like it."

"He'll be obnoxious."

They walked through the dining room, their arms around each other, and it seemed such a natural thing to do; so like the days when Peter had come down from West Point, so like the days on Governors Island, when they had streaked out to raid the refrigerator, that Tippy stopped at the door and said, "I don't feel as if you'd ever been away."

"I don't, either. By tomorrow, the year in Texas will be a dream and all the years here the reality."

"We'll go up and charge around West Point tomorrow, and see Bobby." Tippy swung open the door, and the fuss Trudy made over Peter was drowned out by the yelps of joy Switzy gave his beloved.

CHAPTER III

"GREAT day in the morning!" Tippy cried excitedly, sitting cross-legged on the living-room floor, her pleated skirt making a blue island on the gray sea of rug. "What a wedding we're going to have!"

On her lap she held a box tied with a wide satin bow, one of the many wedding gifts that kept the parcel post and express trucks busy, and Peter said ruefully, "It look as if the Jordon contingent will fill up most of the church. Jordons seem to be pouring in from all directions."

He was comfortable in his army slacks and black West Point sweater with its large gold-and-gray A on the front, and his hair was neat and smooth against her feathery curls as he sat down beside her and bent over to help her loosen the knot. "Who'd ever have thought that Dad could stage a conference in Washington on the very week his son plans to be married?" he said, yanking the beautiful satin she wanted to save, in a way that only tightened and rumpled it. "Or that Jenifer and her husband would want to fly all the way over from England and bring Donny and Bitsy?"

"Or that Gwenn and Bill could bear to leave their glamorous Hollywood." Tippy stopped fooling with the white rosette and rested her elbow on the box, her chin cupped in her hand. "Won't it be wonderful to have the Jordons all together again?" she asked dreamily. "All of them. Even Susan and Neal and Vance, out of school. And aren't we proud to be the ones who are causing the reunion?"

"You bet."

The Jordon family was so large and complicated. General Jordon had managed to rear three sets of motherless children, his own, his second wife's, the three who were theirs together, plus an orphaned nephew. And at one time, before some of them grew up and married, he would march them off to church like a squad of soldiers. He always stalked along at the head of the column, with Jenifer, his faithful little aide-de-camp, and Peter his loyal sergeant, a step or two behind him, with little Vance dragging the toddling Bitsy at the end of the line, as fast as her short legs would go. "Quite a showing, eh?" he would yell proudly at any neighbors who happened to be watching.

"You know," Peter said, remembering that and amused now at the blushing embarrassment it used to cause him, "I'll be glad to see the clan together again. But," and he stretched his long legs out and leaned back on his hands, "I wish it didn't have to be right when I'm getting married. It's so complicating. Where are we going to bed 'em all down?"

"Jenifer and Cyril will stay at David's," Tippy said, repeating the arrangements she and her mother had made the night before. "Now that David's back in the army again for this queer kind of war we're in and stationed right in New York, Lord and Lady Carlton will be entertained in the style to which Jenifer's become accustomed—a real English butler, and everything.

Oh, I know it doesn't matter a hoot to her," she laughed, "but it is nice that Carrol's so rich and Gladstone's such a beautiful estate and has room for so many people. Bitsy, and Donny, and. . . ."

"For heaven's sake don't shove Gwenn and her movie hero in on them," Peter interrupted, worried. "She'd wreck it for everyone."

"Silly. Just Bitsy and Donny are going to be there, and maybe Vance. The twins will stay at Penny's, and when Alice and Jon come up on the day of the wedding. . . ."

"But where's Gwenn going?" Peter still wanted to know. "Not here, I hope."

"Just your father will be here." Tippy had to laugh at his lugubrious scowl. But she did say to end his misery, "Gwenn and Bill want to stay at the Waldorf. Mums told you that, you dope."

"I can't listen to everything—in my nervous condition." He heaved a vast sigh of relief and grinned at her. "Jenifer's married to an all-round guy, the future Earl of Easterbrook, and they'll fit in at Carrol's and be swell, but I can't say the same for Gwenn. She's a nut who married a nut. I suppose Bill thinks the photographers can find him quicker if he stays in town."

"Gwenn said that on the telephone to Mums."

"Then by all means, let's leave her there." Peter's family was disposed of, not entirely to his satisfaction but with a minimum of inconvenience to the ones who would have to entertain so many, so he poked at the box again. "Time's wasting," he said, both to remind Tippy of the gift and a note of thanks to be written, and to forget that Gwenn would shortly stir things into a tempest. She always had and she always would.

But Tippy scrambled up. "Did you hear the boys fighting?"

she asked anxiously, running to the window. "Oh, dear, Switzy's being horrid again!" And she streaked back to jerk open a French door.

Peter sat where he was. Rollo could take care of himself. And when he heard her shout from the side porch, "Switzy, stop that this minute! Shame on you!" he only grinned. Rollo was a kindly old gentleman but his teeth were sharp. There was a limit to his patience, too, and Peter listened to a surprised yelp and flying feet patting the length of the porch. A gust of wind blew tissue paper about the floor as two furry bodies flung themselves inside and across his legs, and Tippy banged the door shut.

Switzy shrieked his way to the kitchen, but Rollo stopped and flopped down.

He looked like an old gray mop someone had thrown on the floor. Two beady eyes peeped out at Peter and the duster end wagged cheerfully. "The silly thing," he seemed to say, "I didn't hurt him." Then he smiled contentedly and gave sweeping licks at Tippy's hand as she knelt down to feel for wounds in his fur.

"He's O.K.," Peter told her calmly. "He isn't quite as big as Switzy but he's had a lot more fights and he's tougher."

"Do you think they'll keep this up forever?"

"Probably. Didn't you and Bobby ever mix it up?"

"All the time. Bobby always started it and I came out with bumps that made him ashamed. Switzy," she said, giving Rollo a pat and sitting down on the carpet again, "is very much like Bobby—a show off."

"And a really nice guy. How about going to see my pal this afternoon?"

"And take him a cake." Tippy loved her brother far more than she let others know, and she confided now to Peter, "He's such a happy moron. I'm glad you chose him to be your best

44

man. Since Gil MacKettrick's in Korea and can't come, I'm glad you chose Bobby. Of course it would have been nicer to have your roommate, but Bobby's awfully proud."

"I'd really rather have him."

"And I'll have Alcie. Oh, Peter," a glass bowl stayed hidden in its box while Tippy leaned over and said softly, "it's all working out so *right*."

"Just four more days," he answered, drawing her nearer. "Then we'll be married, with just one more day to go before we're off on a boat."

"With all smooth sailing. All by ourselves, with our whole life before us. Why," she said, turning to look at him, "we'll be like all the other couples. We'll have problems: unpacking our luggage and wondering if the car is safely on board, and if the boys are all right, down in the kennels, and if our barrels of wedding gifts and sheets and blankets are in a safe place, and what kind of house we'll have."

"And hoping we won't be seasick." Peter pulled her over and kissed her. "Are you a good sailor, madam?' he asked practically.

"I'm one of the best." Tippy straightened up indignantly, then stared at him with her golden eyes wide. "Why, we don't know each other!" she cried with sudden panic. "We don't know anything about each other. How can I possibly go off with someone I don't know?"

"Good grief, you know me like a book. Or if you don't, you never will," he returned, amused, but seeing the little pulse that throbbed wildly against her throat. "You know mushrooms poison me, and that I keep my room in pretty good shape and never crab about giving up my turn for the car—my sisters always got it anyway—and you know I spill ashes around and like to stay up late, and have the radio news with my morning coffee. What surprises me," he said with sudden seriousness, "is that, knowing all these things about me and having seen me around for six years, you'd take me on at all."

"Or that you'd want me with all my foolish notions. I guess it's all right." Tippy sighed and relaxed. "As the day comes nearer, I keep having jumpy ideas and butterflies. Just nerves, I guess."

"And rushing so fast." Peter pulled the crystal bowl from its nest and held it up to the light. "Nice," he said, "from the Shipleys." And he reached behind him to set it on a table. "We're going for a drive," he announced. "Away from the hurry and confusion. No more clothes will be bought today, no tearing into town and back, no telephoning. We'll drive up to West Point and lunch at the hotel, the way we used to do. We'll go for a stroll along Flirtation Walk and get acquainted again."

"But, Peter. . . ."

"No buts. Up you go."

Before she could resist she was on her feet, and even while she pleaded to make just one or two important telephone calls, Peter had changed his sweater for his blouse and had bundled her into her bright red coat.

"We're off," he said, shaking his head at Rollo who sat staring up expectantly. "No dogs." And Rollo went off and lay down. But Switzy cried through the pantry door.

"Maybe we should take them," Tippy suggested, straightening the little red cap he had squashed down on her head. "They wouldn't be any trouble."

"This is the bride's day," he answered, taking his own short-coat from a hanger and shrugging into it. "Her relaxing day. It's also the only day the groom will really see the bride, for tomorrow he has to deliver his car to the boat and his family begins trickling in. This is our get-to-know-each-other-again day."

46

"Then let's begin it."

Tippy was eager now. She gave her cap a pat and danced to the door, to say saucily over her shoulder, "Who cares about a little thing like a wedding? Somebody will buy me more luggage today or I'll borrow that huge trunk of Penny's, or maybe pack my clothes in a box." And she called upstairs blithely, "Bye, Mums. I'm going AWOL, so hold the fort.

"Um, it smells fresh and good," she said outside, sniffing in great breaths of cold air. "Shall we stop by and thank Carrol for the big family party she's giving us, the night after our wedding?" she asked. "And tell her Gwenn won't be staying there?"

"Who's day is this?"

"Ours."

She hooked her arm through his and pulled him down the steps with her. "It seems to me that you're kind of bossy," she laughed, when she was on the wide seat and could sit sideways, her feet tucked under her. "You used to wait for me to make up my mind. You used to ask, 'What would you like to do, Tippy?' Of course I never knew, but you used to ask. Now you just boss me all the time, and hustle me into restaurants when I'm busy, and make me come home when I'm not half through my shopping."

"I wonder why." Peter leaned over to start the motor and winked at her across his shoulder.

"So I'll eat and have plenty of rest," she returned complacently. "Because Mums tells you to." Tippy flounced straight on the seat and told the windshield mirror, "When I'm married I intend to do as I please. I'll be hard to handle. I'll be a—a flying pinwheel."

"And sputter out with a *fzzzz*. I know." The car rolled off and he reached out and pushed her cap down over her nose.

"Well, anyway," she said behind it, illogically and happily, "I'm glad we have a nice car. It's big and fat, but it isn't too far to the back seat. I can reach around and hit the boys just fine from here. One growl out of either of them and, wham, they get it."

"Smoke works better. A whiff of cigarette smoke in Rollo's face shuts him up like a clam."

"Then you'll have to do that, not me. Oh, Peter." She pushed back her cap and flopped around again to look at his fine, firm profile. "I do like you so much," she said. "I love you, but I like you, too. Do you like me?"

"Sometimes. Twenty-four hours out of every day I like you. The rest of the time. . . ." He shrugged.

"And if you ever don't like me, will you tell me so? Will you please say, 'Tippy, I don't like you much right now'? I will. I'll tell you."

Peter nodded, but he wondered how there could ever be a moment when Tippy would irk him. It would be like waking to find the sun burned out and the earth in darkness, or opening a book that had no print. Unbelievable and impossible. It couldn't happen. "I'll like you, nut, no matter what you do."

"But what if we quarrel?" she persisted. "Do you suppose we ever will?

"Hundreds of times." He knew she had been floating on air for ten days and was searching for solid footing. Marriage was real; not just a golden cloud to rest on, drifting leisurely through a rainbow sky. It was more like a well-balanced meal that either kept you healthy or made you push away your plate and starve to death. Golden clouds and whipped cream sundaes couldn't hold their own against a plain blue sky and a dependable menu, savory and well-seasoned. The simile flashed through his mind

48

and he wished he could express it aloud. He did say, though, "We don't expect to always agree with each other, but we'll work things out together. Love takes care of it, honey."

"That's good," she said with satisfaction, her doubts gone now and enjoying this novel advance on marriage. "But just the same, I think I'll wear high heels most of the time."

"Why?"

"So I can be tall and impress you. I can't ever get to be six-foot-one, like you, but I can be a lot more impressive in high heels." Then she began to laugh. "Whoever heard of people planning to quarrel before they were married?" she asked.

"They'd be better off if they did," he answered. "It's bound to happen. We expect to be exposed to colds and have money problems, so we prepare for such things. Why shouldn't we put bottles of understanding and common-sense pills in our medicine cabinet, along with cough syrup and a reserve fund in the bank?"

"Why, Peter, you're positively astounding! How could you learn all this?" she asked, wide-eyed.

"By living. By watching friends of mine who snap at each other in public, by wanting so much to be married to you and thinking how well we could run a life together."

Tippy leaned over and laid her cheek against his shoulder. "I don't believe I could ever be mad at you," she said softly.

"I'm stubborn."

"So am I."

"When I think I'm right an atom bomb can't move me."

They laughed together until she sat up again to say ruefully, "My trouble is—I never know just *when* I'm right. Somebody, usually Mums or Trudy, has to tell me. And then I don't always believe it. If they say, 'You're right about that, Tippy, so stand up for yourself,' I go wobble-kneed and have to be propped up. But if one of them says, 'Child, you're wrong,' bless me, I'm ready for battle."

"I'll avoid all use of the word."

He slowed the car for a small village, and said as they rolled along its main street, "I'll simply suggest, in a very kind way, 'My dear, do you think you could be mistaken?' "

"And I'll throw one of our wedding presents at you." She found a lipstick in her coat pocket and pulled down the sunshade on the windshield. "Chatting with you is very educational, Lieutenant," she said, studying her face in the mirror on the back of the shade, deciding her lips were red enough, and pushing it up again. "I think being married to you will be even nicer. There's your old school, chum."

The open gates of West Point loomed ahead of them. A sentry came out of his box to return Peter's salute; and as they went along the wide street each had traveled so many times before, Peter said, "It feels strange to come back as an officer. I took my first salute at that gate, the day I graduated, and I thought I'd never get my hand up to my cap."

"And now it's easy. It's like our wedding will be," she said with sudden understanding. "We've been riding along, planning about it, figuring things out and calming our nervous butterflies, and someday we'll look back on it and say, 'Weren't we funny?' Where are we going first?"

"Are you hungry?"

"Not yet."

"Then let's catch Bob before he goes to mess hall. I can go in barracks and snag him off before formation. He'll have a few minutes."

"Five will be enough," Tippy said flatly.

She sat in the car while Peter disappeared inside the great

square quadrangle that was banned to the feminine world. Cadets formed for classes there, marched their penalty tours, or walked across its stone area, solving their personal problems. And when she saw two familiar figures come back through the archway, olive drab and West Point gray together, she jumped out of the car and flung herself at the gray one.

"Stop hugging me!" Bobby Parrish growled, clutching his cap. "Not in *public*."

He gave her a squeeze before he pulled away, so Tippy hung onto him and cried happily, "I'm so excited. I haven't seen you for weeks and weeks, and Mums will ask me how you look. Stand still."

She peered up into his bright blue eyes and nodded. "O.K.," she said, wishing she looked more like Bobby, cocky and determined. "You're still the thinnest thing alive, but you're handsome."

"Shut up." He jerked loose from her, then, without caring how many cadets might be looking out of their windows, he kissed her. "Happy landings, kid," he said. "I'm for this mission a hundred per cent. I'll be home on Friday to take command of it."

"Heaven help us!"

Tippy was pleased with the kiss. She was always pleased with any attention Bobby showed her, even when it cost her money and meant changing her previous plans, but she never let him know it. "I suppose," she said, as he pushed her toward the car with the flat of his hand against her back, "you'll have a date next Sunday night and will want to bring her to Carrol and David's party."

"Nope. No dates. Not until after you sail on Monday. I shall devote my time exclusively to the family, and especially to Lieutenant and Mrs. Jordon."

He set his cap straight with such an inscrutable look in his eyes that Tippy asked anxiously, "Bobby, you aren't planning to play any tricks, are you? You won't throw rice and embarrass us at the ship?"

"Who knows? Take her away, Peter. See you Friday." A comradely thump hit Peter's chest as Bobby strode away in a military exit, but he spoiled the whole effect by turning to demand, "Where's my usual cake?"

"Trudy didn't send it. You can have a piece of mine from the wedding," Tippy shouted. "You can put it under your pillow and dream on it—probably of Theo."

"Or a couple of other *femmes* I've met this year. So long."

Tippy watched his arm go up in a wave, then shook her head at Peter. "Now I wish you hadn't asked him to be your best man," she said. "He'll do something awful, I know he will. Just when I'm feeling sorry for him, because he has to stay up here and go marching around without any privacy or fun of his own, he does something that makes me mad. He *pushed* me!" she cried.

"My dear, don't you think you could be mistaken?" Peter's mouth widened in a grin as he quoted his own light words, and she leaned against the car and laughed.

"No, I don't," she returned, "but it doesn't matter. You're bigger than he is, and you can fight him for me. Let's go to the club and have some lunch. I'm starved."

CHAPTER IV

JORDONS were everywhere.

Packing dresses in her room, Tippy could hear some of them downstairs. General Jordon's voice rose above the others, for he rarely spoke—he boomed. He was like a big bear with a shock of gray hair; and had she not known him so well, she might have been intimidated by his gruffness and the sudden way he had of peering at people over his glasses, his eyes keen and searching under their shaggy brows. He was talking now to the twins, Susan and Neal, whose replies were few and inaudible. When they could be heard at all, they came out in a hesitant murmur that had to be clarified by a younger brother, Vance. He provided a shrill and determined treble to his father's bass.

Tippy dropped a new straw hat on the bed and ran along the hall to say at the door to Peter's room, "I just thought of something. What if I hadn't known you for a long, long time? Why, I'd be scared to death. Suppose I had to meet such a big family all at once? What if they'd arrived here in a body and I hadn't known them before?"

"You'd have started running and never come back." Peter stopped his own packing and held out a pair of heavy shoes. "Help me with these," he pleaded, more concerned with his own dilemma than Tippy's imagined one. "I can't find another inch of room."

"I'll take them," she offered, feeling prewifely and helpful. "I'll squash them in one of my cases."

"But remember to put them where we can get at them. I'll be given a job on the ship, you know."

The shoes were high, laced, tanker's boots, the kind an armored force officer uses to tuck the bottoms of his trousers neatly into, to keep them out of a tank's machinery or the mud; and Tippy let them weight her down when she took them. "They'll be cozy in with my hats," she said, straightening quickly because Peter was bending to kiss her.

The top of her head met his chin with a crack that clicked his teeth together. "Oh, dear," she said, and whacked him on the back with the boots as she flung her arms around him.

"Hey!" he yelled. "Don't knock me out. I'm being married tomorrow." He pretended to sway in a groggy circle until she pushed him down into a chair.

"Pooh," she said, and departed with her boots.

She was so happy. She wanted to sing and do a dance in the upstairs hall. And when Peter called, "Don't forget we're due at Fort Hamilton at one o'clock for our tetanus shots and the orientation class," she caroled back, "Umhum, I know."

The lopsided conversation was still going on downstairs, so she paused to listen. Susan and Neal were telling of their year in boarding schools; at least she supposed they were, for General Jordon was booming out questions and monosyllabic answers came at the end of them. Tippy could almost see the squirming going on as the secret lives of the twins were spread out like nondescript rugs for the General to tramp back and forth on. Vance took his turn and did better. He piped out such tales of prowess that his father could think of nothing to say but "Well, well, well." Tippy set down the shoes and backtracked to Peter.

"Invite a couple of little cadets to come upstairs," she whispered. "The going's getting pretty rough below; and so far as I can tell, the conversation is exactly where it was an hour ago. I don't think your father knows how to end it. I'll take care of Susan."

She returned to the banister, to lean over it and call, "Susan? Are you too busy to come up and help me a little?"

The rush of flying feet was all the answer she needed. Susan swung around the archway and took the steps two at a time. She was a tall girl, for fourteen. Looking down on her, Tippy thought she was more like Gwenn than any of the other Jordons. She had wide, high cheekbones and her eyes were electrically blue.

Gwenn's eyes were like that. They held none of the soft, dark gray that made the eyes of most of the Jordons—Peter and Jenifer, Alice and little Bitsy—seem deep and bottomless. Gwenn stared at people with a hard blue gaze.

"Thank goodness!" Susan cried, tossing back her yellow hair and plunging around the newel post. "Daddy had us almost crazy."

Tippy laughed as they walked along the hall together. Susan might look like the haughty Gwenn, but she had a frank, friendly grin and a rushing little way of saying things.

"I'll help you pack," she offered eagerly. "Just show me what you want me to do. I'm a whizz at putting things in," she said, taking a quire of tissue paper from the bed and sliding off a sheet of it. "I ought to be, I live in a trunk. First it's school, then camp, then school again, with trips in between for holidays at Alcie's or at some of the girls'. What a life. Shall I puff up some of the sleeves of these dresses?"

Her voice held no rancor, only acceptance of her life; and

Tippy pushed a pile of clothes aside to sit down and ask, "Do you mind not having a home, Susan?"

"I hate it." Tissue paper rustled as it was wadded together and thrust into a sleeve, but Susan only shrugged and said matter-of-factly, "There's nothing else to do—not yet, not till I'm older."

"Would you rather live in England with Jenifer, the way Bitsy does?"

"What would I do without Neal?" Susan's grin flashed out as she wadded up another ball of paper. "You see, being a twin's different," she said. "You're really two people."

Tippy thought of Neal downstirs—stamping up the stairs now, really, straight and stiff in his tight gray uniform—and wondered what comfort he could possibly be. From the little she had seen of him, before he had been whisked off to Penny's the night before, he had seemed a pale edition of Susan, whom he constantly brushed out of his way. If his frown meant tenderness, then he loved her dearly. If his constant expression of "Oh, cut it out, slug" meant fatuous interest, then he hung on her every action.

"He's working things out for us," Susan said, as if she read Tippy's conclusion. "He's going to ask Daddy to let him go to a school next year that has both boys and girls in it, instead of to a military academy. He's awfully sorry for me because at least he has Vance to talk to and I haven't anyone."

"Oh, I didn't know that."

"Most people wouldn't. I guess you have to be a twin to know." Susan's hands were deft, and she laid the dress on the other bed, spread paper along its skirt and folded it neatly. "This is ready to pack," she said.

There was nothing of Alice about her. Tippy wished there were, that they could talk as she and Alice always had, even as she and Penny rattled on together. They would soon be sisters. "Susan," she began tentatively; and Susan straightened up with her straight, cool stare. "Would you like to come to Panama for a visit, next summer?"

"I don't know." A tight little shrug was an expressive answer, followed by neither acceptance nor refusal. "I'd have to wait and see what Neal's plans are," she said. "But thank you."

The "thank you" came out with a smile. Tippy remembered the happy little girl on Governors Island who always had a tear in her jeans and a ribbon loose on one of her pigtails. She always skated with a crowd of boys, jammed in with the pack, or was the highest one in a tree, screaming with the rest of them. Life had done something unkind to Susan. It had given her loneliness instead of carefree, childish freedom. Tippy got up and laid both hands on the straight, thin shoulders. "I love you a lot, Susie," she said. "I'm going to love you right along with Penny and Carrol and Alice. I want you to be my sister, too. I want a great big family."

Susan's arms hung straight at her sides. "Thank you," she said with that look of Gwenn's. "I don't know you very well but I'd be glad to love you."

"And we're friends? The way Alcie and I are?"

"I guess so." Susan turned her back, and Tippy thought she heard her mumble, "I sure could use a friend," but she was busy at the bed again. "I'm glad . . ." she said, and swallowed, ". . . that Peter's going to marry you. I've prayed about it ever since he came down to camp to see me this summer."

"Oh, have you, Susie?" Tippy sat down and pulled her new little friend into the welter of dresses.

"Neal prayed, too," Susan went on, "but Vance said we were silly. He said Peter's better off to stay a bachelor." She tried to laugh through her embarrassment, but Tippy hugged her.

"Let's leave this job until Mums comes home," she suggested. "She'll help us. How about you and Neal driving out to Fort Hamilton with Peter and me, then going to the airport with us to meet Jenifer's plane?"

"Oh, Tippy, I'd love to." Her face lighted up and made her look like the little Susan again as she confided, "I've been terribly worried for fear no one would remember to ask us. Neal said. . . ."

"You're asked." Tippy gave her a hug that won her a faithful follower and a tireless little maid-in-waiting for the next few days, and she asked impulsively, "Susan, do you have a long dress?"

"I've a new pink formal that Alcie bought me."

"Then you can be in my wedding. Oh, darling," she said, "I *want* you to be. I was almost fourteen when Penny was married, and I remember what fun it was. Will you do it?"

"Please—please don't be so good to me—it hurts. I'm pretty tough, but it hurts."

Susan bowed her rough head to stare fixedly at her hands, while Tippy resolved to have a private talk with Alcie. She would talk to General Jordon, too, and ask her mother to help her. Little girls were tender things, with tender feelings and tender hearts. This one needed love and security.

"We'll have to make her feel wanted," she said late in the afternoon, back in Trudy's room where Mrs. Parrish was hurriedly fashioning a headpiece that would look something like the bits of tulle and flowers Penny and Alice would wear. "Someone has to do something about her, and no one has. It doesn't seem like Alcie to neglect her. Of course Jenifer's been way off in England and Gwenn wouldn't do anything for anyone, but Alcie should."

"Miss Alcie just got married herself, child," Trudy answered.

"She kept a mighty faithful house till the General went overseas and there wasn't no more house for her to keep. Seems to me this is a papa's duty."

"Well, we've made her happy for the present." Tippy sat down on a low stool and clasped her chin in her hands. "General Jordon can find the kind of school she and Neal want," she decided, "after I talk to Alcie." And she looked up to say, "Jenifer looked lovely, didn't she? She's always so sweet and quiet, and she's kept her American accent. I always think Cyril looks more like a poet or an artist than an earl. He's so dark-eyed and dreamy. Well, they'll all be coming over from Gladstone soon." She stretched her arms above her head, then leaned over to cross them on her mother's knee. "Oh, Mums," she sighed, looking plaintive, "do I have to grow up and get married tomorrow?"

"No." Mrs. Parrish smiled and held the bit of shirred veiling out of harm's way. "We'll turn this into a dress for your doll," she said. "I'm quite sure Peter wouldn't mind waiting another ten years or so."

"Oh, don't let him!" Tippy's hands found each other in supplication. "Don't even *think* such a thing," she begged. "I might lose him. How many are we feeding tonight?"

"Now, let me see." Her mother began to count. "Carrol, David—I wish Penny and Josh could come, but they can't— thirteen Jordons, counting Peter, and our family of course."

"I hope the Gladstone staff is functioning properly down there." Tippy bent her head toward the floor and listened. "I can hear pans rattling," she said hopefully, "but nothing will taste as good as if Trudy had cooked it."

"It'll taste." Trudy had finished Tippy's packing, so she sat comfortably in her low rocker, a little lost at being so idle, but enjoying this quiet hour with the two she loved. Tippy's curls shone from their fresh shampoo, and she wanted to reach out and stroke them. She wanted to hold Tippy there against her mother's knee, pressing them together and hovering over them like a guardian angel; but she only said practically, "It'll soon be time for that boy to come."

"My soul, the great Robert arrives." Tippy jumped up and groaned. "Here goes my peace and quiet," she lamented. "I'll send him up here as soon as Dad brings him, and in the meantime, I'd better send up Susan. Will you fit the flowery crown on her head?"

"It's nearly ready."

Mrs. Parrish bent over her work, while Trudy rocked and watched Tippy run down the hall. "Seems like our child can't relax and be happy without worryin' over the rest of the world," she said, prophetically. "She's goin' to get herself all worked up and troubled over that little Susan. Right here at her weddin' time, too. She ought to be joyful."

"Girls never are when they're about to be married," Mrs. Parrish answered, biting off her thread and holding up her work. "They're too emotional. Perhaps it's better for Tippy to worry over poor Susan than over leaving us." She shook the flowered wreath with its full tulle veiling and said, "I have a feeling we're going to have tears before we're through, Trudy."

"I knows it."

"None of our children have married and gone so far away, and neither David nor Penny was ever as dependent on us as Tippy is. She'll come through the wedding beautifully, but, oh, I do dread Monday so."

"Remember when you took her off to Europe to live and she clung to me an' wouldn't go on the ship? I had to read her the riot act to move her at all. David an' Penny was promisin' her everything under the sun they could think of, but nothin' could budge her."

"I suppose you'll have to do it again, on Monday. I can't." Mrs. Parrish sighed and laid the flowers in her lap. "Oh, Trudy, what will we ever do without her?" she groaned, reaching for the brown hand that was always there for comfort.

"There, there, Miss Marjorie," Trudy said softly, patting. "Don't fret. Our baby won't be gone so long."

"I know she won't. I had to go off and leave my mother, but it was all so long ago and it doesn't help to try to remember how we both felt." A little sigh caught in her breath as she said unhappily, "I wonder if Mama's house was as empty as ours will be."

"They always is. What we has to remember, Miss Marjorie, is this." Trudy leaned forward in her chair and said with sweet certainty, "We don't want our child like she was two years ago, when Mr. Ken was killed. No matter how much we miss her, it won't tear our hearts out like knowin' she was cryin' herself to sleep every night. She's happy now."

"I think of that every day. I thank God in His beautiful tenderness every night when I go to bed. I'm grateful every time I look at Peter."

"Then we won't cry. You an' me'll be smilin' in the church an' at the ship."

"We'll be the smilingest couple there."

Mrs. Parrish picked up the little flowered ornament again and looked it over carefully. There was nothing more to do to it, so she laid it on the table beside her. "Loving little Tippy," she said wistfully. "I wish she were Susan's age again."

"Miss Marjory," Trudy scolded, "stop it. What did we just decide?"

"That we're very, very happy. And we are. Now." Mrs.

Parrish stood up briskly and brushed ravelings from her skirt. "What else have we to do?" she asked.

"Nothin', that I knows of. The children took their car to the boat, their 'hold baggage' has been gone a couple of days, and the rest of their bags is packed. The weddin' gifts is gone, too, and all our own weddin' clothes is ready. Seems like there wasn't much for us to do, not with the Officers Club fixin' a fancy reception an' a florist decoratin' the church."

"Dave and I can at least drive in to the Island tonight with Tippy's gown and veil. She's to dress at the Cromwells', so we can leave them there."

"I heard tell Miss Alcie's doin' it. She and Mr. Jon has to take hers somewhere, so they planned to take Tippy's an' Susan's, too."

"Isn't there anything for the bride's mother to do but fidget?" Mrs. Parrish looked dismally at Trudy, but the twinkle was back in her eyes. "Do you know, I think my husband's a very lucky man," she said. "Off he goes to his work, willy-nilly."

"Yes'm." Trudy answered obediently, but she shook her head as she thought about Colonel Parrish. " 'Tain't the kind of work he likes, though," she said. "I heard him tellin' General Jordon so last night, and the General said it wasn't fair for such a fine army man to be wounded and retired, right in his prime. He said the army suffered a terrible loss."

"I'm glad the army knows it." Mrs. Parrish nodded up and down with satisfaction. She started for the door then turned and came back. "Trudy," she said, "the children grow up and leave, but I still have Dave. What does anything matter, even the children going their separate ways, so long as I have him? Nothing else counts. I know you understand what I mean because you lost your own young husband when you'd been married such a little while."

"Yes'm, I understand." Trudy sat with her hands folded in her lap, thinking back to the life she might have had; but she looked up to say with her sweet, loving smile, "There never was a better man than Colonel Parrish. You'se a lucky woman, Miss Marjory."

"And I know it." She heard the front door open and close, and went running along the hall. "Dave!" she cried, dashing down the stairs as fast as Tippy could have skipped.

First classman Robert Parrish, who had entered with his father, looked annoyed. He thought he should be the important one who was coming home; and when his mother stayed hidden behind a tweed overcoat too long, he tweaked her sleeve. "I'm here, too," he said plaintively. "Here's your little boy."

"Why, so it is." Her arms stayed lifted and quickly transferred themselves to him. "I just had to hang on to Dad a minute," she whispered. "I'm a little tearful, you know. It's Tippy's last night at home."

"Sure. Where's the cause of all the commotion?" Bobby gave her a hearty, understanding kiss and set his cadet cap on her head.

"Probably dressing for dinner."

Gaiety and life came in with Bobby; they always did. And when he strode to the living-room archway, resplendent in his gray overcoat with its cape and shiny buttons, two little cadets hopped up and stood at attention. "And who might these young gentlemen be?" he asked, sounding like a tactical officer on inspection.

"Cadet Jordon, Neal, sir," Neal answered for the pair, "and Cadet Jordon, Vance."

"At ease, men."

The two relaxed ever so slightly, just enough to wrinkle their blouses a little, not quite sure whether they should sit and look like guests again or stay as he left them, for his gaze had shifted to Susan. "My goodness to Betsy," he said, and shot his eyebrows up as high as they would go.

Susan took his stare for a compliment, almost as good as a whistle, and an embarrassing blush spread over her cheeks. "Hello, Bobby," she managed to say with some dignity. "I'm Susan."

"Well, blow me down, so you are. What do you know!" He liked staring at Susan. Being Bobby, he liked staring at all three and making them as uncomfortable as he could before he turned them into slaves. "O.K., men," he said at last, taking off his grin and looking stern. "My gear's out in the car. Double time it."

"Yes, sir."

A rush of air fanned past him, and he caught the smaller cadet and ruffled its shock of black hair. "Off with my overcoat first," he said.

"Yes, sir."

"And the blouse. And bring back a white shirt out of my dresser drawer and the sport coat out of my closet. You may choose me a tie from the rack on the door."

"Yes, sir." Vance divested Bobby of his outer and upper garments, with a tug here and a pull there, and looked like an animated clothes tree when he had finished. Bobby stood in his undershirt.

"This is the way to do it," he said, grinning at his parents. "No use walking upstairs."

Susan had disappeared like a well-trained parlor maid, leaving him nothing pretty to look at while he waited, so he sat down and watched Trudy march in with a small plate of cookies.

"You'se always hungry," she said, just as if she had seen him yesterday. "Supper's apt to be a little late, your lordship. It ain't proper for you to sit around in just your shirt an' pants, an' it might have been politer if you'd gone upstairs to speak to General Jordon an' Peter. They's the important guests, not you. Though we's always delighted to have you."

"Um."

She looked down at her plate in surprise. It was empty; and Bobby wasn't even chewing. "What you done with the cookies so quick beats me," she said, and would have turned away but he choked and a shower of crumbs shot out. "You crazy boy," she said fondly. "Ain't you ever goin' to quit your foolishments?"

"Um-um." The cookies were a crumbly mass in his mouth and he had to chew them somehow. His fresh attire had arrived by the time he could talk, so Trudy left him knotting his tie in the mirror over the mantel and sending Vance on more errands.

"He's somethin'," she said to Mrs. Parrish who was inspecting the dining room table, set with stacks of plates, napkins, knives and forks for a buffet supper. "All the flowers in the living room stood up straighter in their vases when he come in. The roses opened out like the sun had started shinin' an' the fire perked up an' started to burn better. He's the beatin'est child."

"It's lucky the other three aren't like him," Mrs. Parrish returned with composure. "We'd have all gone quietly mad long ago."

Mrs. Parrish understood Bobby; and when he came up behind her and nuzzled his chin along the side of her neck, she reached back to smooth his unruly curls. They felt comforting and rough. "Kind of low, huh?" he asked, clasping his hands around her waist.

"Just a little."

"Dad is, too, but you needn't be. The kid's O.K. We've got a good man in Peter. He'll look after her, Mums."

"I'm sure he will, Bobby."

"I'll explain her to him as soon as I can. I guess I understand Tip better than anyone, since I've practically reared her. You might even say that all she is, she owes to me. Mums—" he turned her around to face him—"I'm just trying to be a little bit jolly," he said solemnly. "How about remembering what you used to say to us kids? 'Smile up your face.' "

Mrs. Parrish had to laugh. "Oh, Bobby, darling, you're priceless," she chuckled, hugging him. "You hate losing Tippy almost as much as I do, don't you?"

"Yes, darn it."

"Then trot upstairs and tell her so. Quick, before all the people from Gladstone come. And please," she begged, giving him a pat, "be kind. Don't tease her."

She listened to him mounting the stairway, slowly, as if planning a campaign on every step, and wondered if he were practicing a beginning. "What a funny boy he is," she told the table.

~~~~~~

CHAPTER V

~~~~~~

"Is anybody paying any attention to the time up there?" Bobby shouted from the bottom of the stairway. "Are you planning to have a wedding, or aren't you? It's darned near five o'clock."

"We're almost ready." Mrs. Parrish leaned over the banister and shook her finger at him. "If you upset Tippy," she warned, "she'll never finish dressing."

"Why not? Peter and his father left ages ago. It seems to me," he contended hotly, "if the groom can get where he's going on time, the bride should make some sort of effort." His mother leaned a little farther out to hush him, caught his attention, and heard his flattering whistle. "Wow!" he said. "Move around where I can see you."

Mrs. Parrish placed herself in plain view and turned slowly for him to admire the graceful folds of her long green dress.

"Gorgeous, but gorgeous," he flattered sincerely. "You'll sure make it hard for the bride. I like the pink feathers on your funny hat, too."

"They're the same little plumes I wore to Penny's wedding," she cupped her mouth to whisper, "just recurled. They're my something old."

"Ver-y neat."

Colonel Parrish came out of his room wearing his full-dress blues, white shirt front and waistcoat starched, gold epaulets so shining that Bobby transferred his attention to him. "It's good to see you back in uniform again, Colonel," he said. "We're a fine military-looking family, and I hope some of your stuff will fit me when I graduate—or David's, when he gets out of the army again. I won't be able to afford a lot of fancy stuff."

"Parrishes always have, son." Colonel Parrish moved aside for his wife to float back the way she had come and looked down at the straight cadet below him. Bobby was agleam with brass buttons. They marched in two rows down his chest and glittered on the tails of his gray dress-blouse. "You might warm up the car," he said, knowing from experience that Bobby reacted unbecomingly to compliments. "Trudy's helping Tippy put the last of her junk in her toilet case, then we're ready."

"Consider it done." Bobby offered a snappy salute as his father turned back to Tippy's room.

Organized confusion seemed to be reaching a climax there, with Tippy dropping combs and lipsticks and Trudy picking them up and putting them into a cosmetic case.

"It seems sort of backwards to be going to my wedding in my traveling suit," Tippy said, buttoning her brown jacket, then unbuttoning it again to feel if she had put on her belt. "I think I packed my brown hat by mistake and sent it to the Waldorf."

"It's on your head."

"Oh. Well, I haven't any purse and gloves. I'll have to hunt them."

She was about to open the empty dresser drawers again but her mother took her firmly by the arm. "Here's your purse," she said, "with your gloves inside. You're all ready now."

There was no further excuse to delay. Tippy picked up her old beaver coat and took one long last look around the yellow-and-green room she was leaving forever. She wanted to remember the little quilted chair with its reading lamp on a table beside it, the flowered spreads, one of them still dented from the nap she had taken, Switzy's wicker basket, the long empty shelf above the bookcase where family photographs had been. "I guess I'll have to go now," she told the room, and followed her mother out.

Downstairs, she found another excuse. While Bobby vented his irritation on the horn and her father let drafts of bitter cold air through the open door, she suggested, just for a final look at the kitchen, "I'd better go out and tell the boys good-by."

"You'll get in the car," Trudy snapped. "The boys, as you call 'em, is havin' their supper. I jus' went out to see 'em, an' it's no use startin' 'em barkin'. They ain't goin' with us. March out."

"All right." Tippy kept her eyes straight ahead as she went meekly out into the early, wintery dusk.

The car heater sent out warmth on the long drive to New York and across the narrow channel of water that separated the world's most famous sky line from a pancake island. Tippy, sitting between her father and Bobby on the orange-and-white ferry that swam across the water like a duck, watched blurred lights on a dock grow larger and clearer through the windshield. She could see a bare, tall flagpole, robbed of its Stars and Stripes by retreat, a wide plaza with a cannon in its center, and a curving road that followed the shore line and led to a chapel beside the Officers Club.

"Aren't you going the wrong way?" she asked Bobby, when they left the ferry and he turned right instead of left.

"Cromwells," he answered, skirting a soldier who had just climbed out of a jeep. "Did you arrange for cars to meet people at the ferry, Dad?"

"All set. They'll meet the seven o'clock, the seven-fifteen, and even the seven-thirty, in case someone is late. Slow down, son, this is the Cromwells' quarters."

The island was so small and it's half circuit so brief, that Bobby swung the car into a circular driveway beside a large brick house. Someone boosted Tippy out and across a lighted porch, into a house where lamps glowed but no one seemed to be at home, and up a stairway into a bedroom.

"Sally thought we'd rather be alone," her mother explained, taking the toilet case from Bobby and closing the door. "Oh, how sweet of her to have a little supper set out for us. Eat something, darling."

Tippy looked at a silver tray on a table and turned away. "Ugh," she said. "I couldn't."

"A little coffee?"

"Later, maybe. I'll eat at the reception. I'll be hungry by then for salad and sandwiches and cake—I hope," she added numbly.

Her wedding dress hung from a side light, its satin folds cascading onto a sheet, the train carefully spread out. Her wedding veil was draped over a special rack the milliner had sent with it, held high and away from the floor, and they seemed to fill the large room.

"Isn't it silly to go to all this trouble?" she asked, looking at them and wondering how she would ever manage so much material and floating tulle. "It's almost barbaric, when I could just walk into the chapel with Peter, in my new brown suit and holding his hand. I seem to have lost him somewhere in all this confusion."

70

"He isn't far away." Mrs. Parrish began divesting Tippy of her jacket as if she were small again, and she said brightly, "For goodness' sake, child, help a little. Don't hit my hat."

"I wish I could see him a minute." Tippy stepped out of her skirt and stood holding it against her white satin slip. "I think," she said plaintvely, "that every bride should see her future husband before she goes in the church. Just so she can see what he *looks* like. I haven't the faintest idea how Peter looks. I keep seeing you and Dad."

"We'll give you a glimpse of him before you go down the aisle." Mrs. Parrish took a circle of net and hoops from the bed and let it drop into a skirt. "Here," she said, determinedly gay. "Put on this contraption, and don't forget about my hat."

Somehow, she got Tippy dressed. With Colonel Parrish's help, she even got her down the stairs and standing in the back of the car. Tippy was docile. She bent patiently over the front seat while they arranged her voluminous trains behind her, spreading them over the sheet.

"I thought I was supposed to have a bouquet," she said, when the doors were finally closed and the heater churning away. "Like the artificial one I used when I had my picture taken."

"Trudy has it at the church," her mother answered. "Dave, drive slowly."

The two dear heads were so close. By holding on and bending a little more, Tippy could put her face between theirs. "I love you both so much," she whispered. "Right at this minute—and it seems awful to say it—I love you more than anyone else in the world."

"Not more than Peter, darling."

"No, but I'm going to *have* Peter. You see," Tippy tried to explain, "I'll have Peter but I'll be losing you. This is a silly time to tell you how much I love you, standing up and all humped over like this, but I have to. I feel as if I'll just die if you don't know it."

"We do know it, Tippy, dear." Colonel Parrish stopped the car by the historic gray stone chapel. Lights shone softly through its stained glass windows and the faint roll of organ music floated out. Women in long skirts with officers or men in evening dress were going up its shallow stone steps as he said, "We understand. You're very close to us."

There was so much he wanted to say, but Tippy was like Bobby, in a way. Compliments ruined Bobby, and too great a show of tenderness would be sure to dissolve her in tears. So he only said, "Let Mums help you out while I go next door and park in front of the club."

"I'll take the car, sir." A young soldier appeared beside the window as if he had popped up out of the ground, and saluted Colonel Parrish. "We have a space reserved for you," he said, and hurried around to open the doors on the other side.

Tippy was handed out like a frosted cake. Her father guided her along the walk while her mother hustled behind with the train. The heavy church doors opened to louder swells from the organ, and a cluster of people in the vestibule turned expectantly.

"Hello, cherub," Penny said, lovely in rose chiffon. "I didn't think I could do it, but I beat you here. I wish I didn't have to run the minute it's over."

Tippy wished she didn't, too. She searched for words to tell Penny so, but so many others crowded around her. There was Peter's sister, Alice, just as lovely in a paler shade of rose, and something pink that must be pretty little Susan. There were the ushers, too. Tippy tried to sort them out. Never had she seen people move around so much, offering their arms to ladies who were late, side-stepping men who mumbled their apologies. She couldn't tell who was in the wedding party and who wasn't, and besides, she couldn't see very well through her veil.

"Were's Trudy?" she asked, taking a good peek to be sure she was talking to Alice.

"David took her inside. Carrol's in there with her and they're sitting together."

"But she has my flowers."

"They're right over here." Alice produced a bouquet, much larger than the one Tippy had expected. It was round and compact, made up of white lilies and roses, with floating streamers of narrow white satin ribbon.

"Peter really outdid himself," she said, taking it and beginning to remember Peter, who was also a part of all this, seeing exactly how he must have looked when he solemnly selected the flowers. She couldn't fit him into this fluffy, whispered confusion, and she asked, "If I open the door a crack could I look at him?"

"Not yet." Alice adjusted the bouquet in Tippy's cold hands. Her straight brown hair swung forward before she looked up from under her brown bang and wisp of tulle ruffle. "He won't come out of that little room he's in until Bobby brings him," she said.

"Then where's Bobby?"

"Seating people."

"He shouldn't be. My goodness," Tippy cried, awake at last and outraged, "it's time for the wedding to start! This is a *wedding!*" She suddenly discovered herself to be in the middle of a performance, something like the dramas she had staged for television. It had to go off on schedule. People in her audience might start to fidget. And there was Penny's play to think of. Penny had a first-act curtain to make. "Really!" she said, exasperated. "What time is it?"

"We have three minutes yet," her father answered. "Don't be nervous, honey. Mums has to be taken down the aisle first, before we start, you know."

As if on cue the inner doors pushed open and Bobby looked in. "Why don't we go?" he asked, echoing Tippy's question. "I'll take Mums now."

"You'll do nothing of the sort." Tippy disarranged her flowing robes to step forward and scold, "Why, you're supposed to be with Peter. You shouldn't leave him all by himself."

"But who'll take Mums?"

"Someone else will. David."

"David's sitting down in the front pew beside Carrol, just as if he didn't have a darn thing to do."

"Then Josh will, or Jon, or Neal."

"Mums would look like heck leaning on Neal."

Bobby stepped inside, and as the door slipped shut Tippy shook her bouquet at him. "If you'd just go attend to what *you* have to do," she cried hotly, "the rest of us could manage for ourselves. I think it would be very nice for Dad to take Mums in, then come back for me. We'll do that if David doesn't show up. But, for goodness' sake, *go away!* Go take care of Peter like you're supposed to do. Why—why he might *faint*, or something. He's as nervous as I am. Wouldn't you know it?" she swung around to say helplessly. "Wouldn't you know I'd have to get into a fight with Bobby at my very own wedding?"

"He's trying to help, dear." Her mother watched Susan straighten the satin folds again; and the door opened against Bobby's back.

"Your cue's about to sound, Mums," David said, shoving Bobby aside. "The same *Ave Maria* you always march in by. The ushers are all through and ready to go." Then his eyes fell on his brother. "Holy smoke," he said. "What are you doing here? Don't you know where you're supposed to be?"

"I'm just going there."

Bobby slid through a crack that was left unguarded, away from David's stern glare and the satisfaction he knew Tippy would be happy to show him. "Well, anyhow, I stiffened her up," he consoled himself, skirting the pews and finding a small door near the flower-banked altar.

He saw Neal and Vance lighting the last of the tapers tied with white satin bows and set in tall wooden candlesticks along the wide center aisle. The organ swelled into *Ave Maria*, and he felt it was high time he attended to his groom. "Sorry, Peter, I didn't mean to neglect you," those in the front rows heard him say, before he shut himself off.

Tippy, left unnerved in the vestibule behind him, watched her mother's straight back walk away from her. The tiny pink plumes bobbed along beside David's gold epaulets, and it was only because David looked so much like her father and covered her mother's hand so comfortingly with his white glove that she could stand where she was. Even so, she wished she had kissed her mother good-by.

Mrs. Parrish was seated. A solemn, expectant hush descended over the church. The organ swelled slowly into the *Lohengrin Wedding March*, and Susan clutched her pink flowers as she left her place in the doorway.

"We—We always have pink w-weddings," Tippy whispered to her father in a voice that sounded far away. "You know—at Penny's, then Carrol's, and m-mine." Alice slipped past her. "S—step—hold—step," she counted, watching. "Alcie does it awfully well, but of course she was married here. I was in her wedding, you know," she chattered. "I was her maid of honor." Penny stepped out and squeezed her trembling hands as she passed. Tippy's eyes followed her and she shook her head. "I—I don't think I—can do it."

"Steady, baby." Colonel Parrish pressed the white sleeve under his arm closer against his side and looked through the gauzy veil at Tippy's eyes asking him for confidence. Two tears clung to her long lashes and he took out his handerchief to lift the veil and carefully dot them away. "We'll just stroll along," he said, returning the handkerchief to his hip pocket and starting them out in step. "When we reach the center of the church, we'll turn and look for Peter."

He wondered if other fathers were ever called upon to put their own loss out of their minds while they reassured the little girl beside them; and when they had made their turn and Tippy whispered miserably, "I can't see him," he answered in a conversational tone, "Oh, you will. The candles make quite a glare, don't they?"

"Y—yes."

Tippy missed a step. "Excuse me," she said in such a small apologetic voice that he squeezed her arm again.

"You're doing fine, just fine," he said in a pleasant monotone, without moving his lips. "We're over halfway there."

"I can't find Mums—oh, I see Peter now. I *see* him." Tippy lifted her head to become a truly beautiful and radiant bride as she passed through the lane of candles, and a little murmur of delight swept over the chapel.

She didn't hear it. She held tightly to her father and kept her eyes on the dear familiar face of Peter. She sent him such a glad, discovering smile that only Bobby's restraining hand stopped him from stepping forward to meet her before it was time.

"Oh, Peter darling," she sighed with relief, when they were safely together, "I thought I'd never get here. It seemed. . . ."

The chaplain was saying something she was supposed to hear, so she turned an obedient head to him.

"Who giveth this woman to be married to this man?" he was asking, and she shifted her gaze to her mother and father. "We do," they answered together, and her father laid her hand in Peter's.

After that she made solemn vows. She made them in two small words aloud, but inwardly she repeated, "I do, oh, I do, I do." She even tried to imitate the proud way Peter answered, but her voice was thin and it broke. There was an unexpected pause in the service. She wondered why the chaplain didn't go on. She held onto Peter while she waited for him to speak, afraid it might be her turn and he was waiting for her, when a sudden tug made her look down. Peter was doing something with a ring and trying to pry her fingers apart. He had red streaks across his knuckles where she had gripped him. She was so appalled at having hurt him that she almost snatched her hand away. But the new gold band was on. Peter looked proud of the achievement.

Someone had taken her flowers away, and now she had them back. Someone else was pulling at the extra little piece of veil over her face and she could see better. She could see Peter better, at least, and some steps she had to go up. There were quite a lot of steps, she counted, four of them, with white cushions at the top.

This is something I'm supposed always to remember, she thought, mounting the steps and pulling her load of train behind her. I'll have to concentrate better if I ever want to talk it over with Peter. Then she knelt down. The chaplain was reading something very beautiful. It was very beautiful and she stopped shaking to listen. It was a prayer, and it was lovely. It gave Peter to her, to keep and to cherish, in the sight of God, forever and ever. She closed her eyes and said a silent prayer of her own. "Thank you, God," she prayed with heartfelt gratitude. "I'll always love him. Always, always."

It was over. She supposed it was over because she was standing up and Peter had kissed her—just as if no people were there at all. And the music was bursting with the same joy she had in her heart. Everyone was smiling.

She swept down the steps and along the aisle. A cameraman caught her winking at her mother as she sailed past, the bridal party streaming out behind her like a long bright ribbon. "I could do it all over again!" she cried in the vestibule. "Oh, I could do it much *better*. I wouldn't have stage fright."

"Not me." Peter stopped pumping hands with the same ushers over and over, two of whom were his classmates, and Josh and Jonathan, to hug her. "Let's get on to the club," he said, "before the mob pours out." But Gwenn was upon him.

Gwenn wore what she called "a simple little thing designed in Hollywood" that took up half the vestibule floor. Sequins on net glittered a brighter gold than her hair, and hoop met hoop as she flung her arms around Tippy. Her husband, not quite tall enough for her splendor but handsome in a bored way, stood by in somber patience until she had finished her effusive embraces.

"Good show," he said Britishly, forgetting Peter had known him as a boy. "Felicitations, Tip, and all that."

He was more English than Cyril, Tippy thought, shaking his limp hand; and she turned from him to young Lard Carlton, who gave her a hearty brotherly kiss before Bobby shouted in his raucous voice, "You'd better run"; and Peter scooped up her train and piled it in her arms.

It seemed just like the old days to her, racing for the club with Peter holding her hand—except for the white bundle she carried. She didn't feel married; she felt young and silly, and as if she were going to somebody's party.

Her flying satin slippers kept pace with Peter's long stride, and they were first under the marquee. They would have been first inside but he stopped to kiss her again.

"We'll be pretty busy from now on," he said, "Mrs. Jordon."

"Smooching." Bobby broke up the kiss and parted them, still the busy master of ceremonies. But he did say with unexpected common sense, "You dopes, it's cold out here. Kiss her indoors where it's warm."

There was no more time for embraces, or even to speak to each other again. Pictures had to be taken: pictures of the bridesmaids and ushers standing in a stiff row on either side of the bride and groom, pictures of Colonel and Mrs. Parrish and General Jordon, flanking Tippy and Peter, and one of the whole large family that took an endless time to pose. Then there was a receiving line to form, with great bustling into place and confusion.

Tippy delayed it. She held up proceedings by declaring in a losing fight, "I don't care what Emily Post says. David and Carrol may not *actually* have been in my wedding, or Jenifer and Cyril or the Hanleys either, but we're a family. Why can't we *all* stand up here together?"

"Because, darling," Carrol pointed out patiently, "we'd stretch all the way across the room. Some of us are needed to talk with the guests. David and I can do that."

Tippy looked at her beautiful sister-in-law. Her heart always smiled when she looked at Carrol. It had a serene, contented feeling that made her give in now and nod. "All right," she said, "but it's a crime for anyone as beautiful as you are to be just walking around on the fringe of things. I didn't think blondes could possibly look so divine in yellow, but you do."

"Thank you, sweet. I'll wear it oftener; David says I should." Carrol was so accustomed to being told she was beautiful that it mattered very little to her. Her perfect features had been a gift at birth, along with unlimited wealth, and she was quite detached from them. David and her two little boys were what counted.

She looked about the large square room that could hold two hundred guests and not be crowded, even with the bride's table in its center, and said smiling, "Jenifer and I can mingle. She'll be glad to see a great many of the Governors Island people again."

A long line of guests was coming up the stairway. Tippy hopped back into her place and Peter leaned close to whisper, "You've been gone a long time."

"I wasn't over a foot away. You could have reached out and touched me," she whispered back. "Why didn't you? Why didn't you yank me back where I belong? Oh, good evening."

"Pay attention, dear," her mother was saying. "Here's Mrs. Vance."

Tippy turned to greet one of her mother's very dear friends. Large brown eyes smiled back at her, and she managed to clasp her bouquet in the crook of her elbow and extend both hands. "It was sweet of you to come to my wedding," she said sincerely, "when it was such a long trip for you."

"I couldn't have stayed away." Mrs. Vance leaned nearer and reminded, "I came to your sixteenth birthday party here, remember? I sat and talked with your mother for a while."

"So you did." Tippy had to juggle her flowers again to pull Peter closer and introduce him. "Peter was here, too," she said.

"I know." Mrs. Vance's eyes twinkled merrily as she told

them both, "I had a premonition that night, that you two would have a wedding someday."

"You did? Oh, wonderful." Tippy was about to confide a secret, but Peter spoke before she could.

"That night was the first time I asked her to wear my A pin," he said with a grin. "The army pin of West Point, you know. She turned me down. She turned me down flat."

"I was scared. I was afraid Bobby would murder me and was sure Mums and Dad would think I'd lost my mind," Tippy defended. "But I did want to take it. I really suffered over passing up that pin."

Other guests were waiting to greet her, so she gave Mrs. Vance's hand a reluctant squeeze. "I'm glad you reminded us of that, tonight," she said, before she began to smile and say "Good evening," over and over again.

There were times during the reception when a vague, puzzling memory floated through her mind. It was something she wanted to remember clearly. The first time it came was when she was opening the dancing with Peter. He held her loosely and they had to be very gay because so many eyes were on them. The orchestra played a Strauss waltz, and as he took her hand, there was a flash of something she wanted to say, then it was gone. The second time came when she was cutting her wedding cake, his hand guiding hers as it pushed the heavy blade down. She almost had it then; but as she looked up to ask whatever it was, a flashbulb exploded. The third time was when she threw her bouquet. Peter lifted her onto the high platform where the musicians sat, and whatever it was, it was right there to read in his eyes as he looked up at her. A semicircle of smiling faces watched her expectantly, girls held out their arms, so she lifted the flowers above her head and threw them straight at Susan. After that it was gone.

Trudy and Alice produced her brown suit and divested her of her cumbersome finery in the powder room downstairs. Paper rose petals sifted down through the cold night air like unseasonal blossoms, and a car borrowed from David whisked her away. Her wedding was over.

CHAPTER VI

THE big chair was very comfortable for two. It held Lieutenant and Mrs. Jordon nicely, and with them the society pages of various newspapers.

"That's me," Tippy said smugly, pointing to a photograph of a bride, the largest of three at the top of a page. "And here's practically a whole column about me—what I wore and who I am and—why, I must have been very important last night. You just got a little bitty paragraph at the bottom."

"Ah, but look at me in this one of us together." Peter laid another paper on top and said with pompous pride, "I'm bigger than you are. I'm walking along, manfully and straight, while you're turning around and winking. Shame on you for winking at one of my groomsmen, the very minute you're married."

"I was winking at Mums." Tippy studied the print again and giggled. She saw a bride and groom leaving the altar under crossed sabers, and she asked, "Did we do that? Walk under an arch of sabers, I mean?"

"We certainly did. Bobby, David, and my two classmates stepped briskly forward in the old tradition. Don't you remember it?"

"I seem to remember some clanking." She slid down against his shoulder and said dreamily, "The whole thing is a complete muddle. I think every bride should be married twice so she can keep her mind on everything—and we didn't even have a rehearsal. Peter, tell me something." She looked up and easily asked the question that had troubled her so last night. "When we were being married, what was I doing to your hand?"

"You had me in a death grip." He bent his head and kissed her, then looked down to tease, "When your father handed you over to me, you hung on as if you were afraid I'd get away. You darned near broke my bones. But we did get the ring on."

Tippy held up her hand and admired the new carved band that matched her gold West Point miniature of Peter's class ring. "I'm the emotional type," she said complacently. "I fall apart in a crisis and clutch at the nearest straw."

"Fine compliment for the man you just married," he retorted, "to be called a straw. And do you have to sit on my hip?"

"I guess so. There isn't any other place." She reached both across him and behind his head to clasp her arms around his neck, and slid down to stretch her legs out as far as she could beside his.

It was an awkward pose that neither could endure for long, and he said above the sleeve of her cashmere sweater, "Let go of me or I'll spill you on the floor."

Her arms came down but her curls stayed nestled under his chin, and she asked seriously, "Peter, how much do you love me?"

"More than anything in the world. More than I can ever tell you."

"Enough to do something nice for me?"

"Anything. Just ask it."

"I've been thinking—while we looked at the pictures—" she pushed against his chest to sit up and regard him anxiously—"about Mums and Dad, a little. Wondering if they're lonesome and wishing they could see me, I mean."

"You'll see them at Gladstone in a couple of hours."

"Yes, I know, but there'll be so many people there. I'm afraid they're lonesome at home. They won't really *see* me before I go away."

"Oh, childie, darling." Peter looked deep into the hazel pools of her eyes, trying to feel as she must feel.

Family meant so little to him; he had been away too long. His father, his sisters and brothers, were relatives to see and enjoy now and then, but his life was a thing apart, his own. Tippy was going off to a new life. In a strange country, miles and miles away. This wasn't just a change of station to her as it was to him, a move to Panama from Texas, made perfect by having a beautiful wife along; it was a whole new future. What if it turned out to be a lonely one, since she had only him to give her happiness?

"I tell you what we'll do," he said, dismissing the fine hotel room where they had been so happy together. "It's too late to pay a call on your parents before we go to Gladstone, because we can't dress and make it in time. But—well, what would you say to packing up our traps and moving out there?"

"You mean—*spend the night?*"

Her small face glowed when he nodded. "We could," he said. "We'd have to get up at the crack of dawn to make the boat, but your family's planning to, anyway."

"In my own room! With Trudy cooking us breakfast and Mums and Dad to drive us in! Oh, Peter!" Her hand scrubbed at her throat as if rubbing the good news in, and she said with a blissful sigh of relief, "I hadn't even thought of anything half so wonderful as *that*. I just wanted to go back for a little while. Just to be alone with Mums and Dad."

"Shall we call them up and tell them we're coming?"

"No, let's keep it a surprise. Let's just leave the party with them and watch them fall in a faint. Oh, darling," she said softly, dropping back against his shoulder again, "you don't think I want to be with them because I'm not happy with you, do you? I wouldn't go back and live there for the world."

"I wouldn't let you." He held her a moment, then slid out of the chair and pulled her to her feet. "Start packing," he said, giving her a spank to send her on her way. "We have to dress for this big affair and we haven't much time."

"I'll slam things in." She began to fold a chiffon negligee with meticulous care and laid it carefully in the smaller case on the luggage racks. "There isn't much to do," she said, putting Peter's pajamas and robe in the other one and running back for her satin mules and nightgown, "since our big bags are already out at the Brooklyn Base and my wedding dress went home in a box."

"I brought more than I needed to." Peter tossed her his leather slippers and exclaimed with pleasure, "Wait a minute. Hold up on mine. I can stay in civilian clothes tonight and put on my uniform tomorrow. Can you squash my blues in, too?"

"I can manage it." She felt important, packing her own and Peter's clothes.

"Then I'll hike down to pay the bill and send a boy up for the bags." He stopped before her with a bright striped necktie in his hand, and she listened in a wifely way while he said, "This isn't a very personal room, is it?"

"It's frightfully city hotelish, but it's nice." She gave the room a satisfied nod and remarked with her hands busy, "It was fun eating there by the window and looking down on all the cold people hurrying to church. I felt very rich."

"And happy?"

"Oh, darling, yes!"

The packing stopped for a few minutes while they told each other how happy they were; then Peter went whistling off to pay his bill and pick up their borrowed car from a garage, and Tippy changed to a sheer black dress and waited for the bellboy to come.

She thanked the room for being so pleasant to them. She even blew it a kiss and told it good-by. And when the door swung shut behind her with a lonesome little sound, she thought she heard it crying.

"We'll come back sometime," she promised, hurrying down to the lobby where Peter had told her to wait for him.

Or *had* he told her there? Had he said the lobby, the Park Avenue entrance, or in the tunneled driveway, one floor below? She couldn't remember.

There was no sign of him or the boy with her bags, for people's belongings aren't allowed to clutter up such a stately place as the Waldorf, and she wondered what to do. Finally she perched on the end cushion of a long, overstuffed divan.

Two elderly ladies in fussy hats and flowing mink coats took up most of the seat. They had come to New York to see the sights, so they disconsolately informed each other, and for all their diamond rings and rich magnificence, they were unhappy. They couldn't buy theater tickets. They couldn't buy them anywhere, not for the play they wanted. Not for Penny Parrish in *A Month of Sundays*, which was the only one they really *had* to see. Tippy listened to them complain in high, chattery voices, and gave a pleased wriggle, until she remembered that she wasn't exactly happy either. Where, oh where was Peter? Why didn't he come to retrieve her?

A page boy passed before the divan and stopped to look at the three. "Mrs. Jordon," he said in a polite voice, to any one of them. "I have a message for Mrs. Jordon." Tippy turned her head to see which of her seat companions might rise and perhaps receive good news about her tickets, but neither did. "Mrs. Jordon," he tried once more before he passed on; and Tippy shot to her feet.

"Oh, my goodness, that's me!" she cried. "I'm——I'm Mrs. Jordon."

"Your car is waiting in the driveway, ma'am."

"Thank you. Oh. . . ." She plowed about in her purse. She knew he was standing there, waiting for a tip, but she had no wallet. Just gloves and a useless compact. No money at all. And she told herself frantically, "Let this be a lesson to you—Mrs. Jordon. Don't ever go off on a honeymoon again, with just a husband. Oh, wait a minute," she said.

There was a fine new address book in the purse with a little pencil attached, and she scribbled hastily on one of its leaves before she turned to the two elderly ladies. "I really am Mrs. Jordon," she told the two upturned pink-and-white faces. "I just got married last night so I'm not quite used to the name yet. But I'm Penny Parrish's sister, too. If you'll please give the boy a quarter for me and telephone this number I've written down, you can have two seats for whenever you want them."

"Why, my dear. . . ."

"And be sure to tell the man who answers that *Tippy* told you to call." She thrust out the paper, watched disbelief turn to amazement, and fled.

Peter had been driving around and around the oval drive-way. Whenever a car stopped to discharge passengers, he hovered behind it until he had to move on; and he was just commencing another lap when Tippy shot through the revolving door and hailed him.

"Oh, I've just had the most exciting adventure," she panted, scrambling in beside him and not waiting for the doorman to assist her properly. "I got lost the very first day I'm married to you and I hadn't any money. I didn't even know my own name," she said, laughing. "I just sat like a lump and might have stayed lost forever. Oh, what if I had!"

"I imagine I might have put the car back into the parking lot after a time and come to hunt for you," he answered, grinning down at her flushed cheeks. "After all I went through to get you, I wouldn't let you stay lost."

"That's a relief." And she began a dramatic account of the abandoned bride on a divan. "What do you suppose the two little old ladies will do?" she ended.

"Pay your quarter and call the number," he answered, chuckling. "What have they got to lose?"

"And won't Josh's manager be surprised! Remind me to prepare Josh for it tonight. Oh, and remind me, too, to take my wallet and travelers checks out of the old brown purse I'm throwing away, and transfer them. I'm always needing money."

"You'd better have some now." Peter let the car coast to a stop for a red light and reached into his trouser pocket. A crumpled five-dollar bill came out and he passed it across to her. "Here, childie," he said, feeling a proud swelling in his chest.

Tippy enjoyed taking it. "It makes me feel so married," she said, waving the bill. "If you'd given me this a week ago I'd have had to pay it back. I'd have been embarrassed. Isn't it funny that walking down an aisle in a long white dress and saying 'I do' can make it all right?"

"It's wonderful. I'm all for it."

Peter started the car again, and Tippy moved nearer on the seat and suggested:

"Let's talk about our wedding again. Let's remember every blessed thing about it."

The remembering lasted until they left the main highway and turned between the gateposts of Gladstone. Far ahead through bare trees they could see the lights of the great house; and as they wound through a park, Tippy said, "It's fun to think that Lieutenant and Mrs. Jordon are going to their first party. Mrs. Jordon. I'm Mrs. Jordon. I have to keep reminding myself because everybody will start calling me Tippy again tonight. I have to be prepared for strangers on the boat tomorrow."

Peter stopped the car before a wide stone terrace. Massive doors opened, letting out a flood of light, as a very correct butler came down a flight of shallow steps.

"Good evening, sir," he said opening the car door as if it were a royal coach. "It was a very beautiful wedding. Be careful of that spot of ice, Miss Tippy."

"Mrs. Jordon," Tippy prompted, letting him hand her out with the dignity he accorded distinguished guests, then looking up with a smile that broke his reserve. "Keep calling me that all evening, Perkins," she coaxed. "Make a point of coming around every once in a while and saying it. It would be so awful if I should forget to answer someone tomorrow. It would look so bridey, wouldn't it?"

"It would indeed, Mrs. Jordon. We must take care that it doesn't occur. If you and the Lieutenant will step inside, a man will take your car. The others are here."

Tippy and Peter looked at each other when they stood in the wide, thickly rugged hall, giving up their hats and coats. "Such richness," she whispered. "They don't even know we're here. At home you can hear a mouse squeak. Shall we enter the drawing room arm in arm, or just bounce in?"

"Let's just get in somehow." He stretched his neck out of his white collar and smoothed his hair. "It's kind of disconcerting," he muttered. "I don't think I ever was a guest of honor before."

"Then take my hand. I'm used to it. I'm the *bride*." And she gave him confidence by saying, "It's just our family, silly. Here we go."

The long room was full of expectant, waiting relatives. When Perkins threw open the double doors they all surged forward, and there was no need for Peter and Tippy to make an entrance; they were surrounded. Children hopped up and down, shrieking and screaming without knowing why, and those who reached the door first felt no concern for the slower ones who were pushed back.

"Help, help, you're choking me," Tippy laughed, with little Parri hanging from her waist and Penny hugging her neck. "Mums, lean closer so I can kiss you."

Peter was thumped on the back and pulled inside. General Jordon boomed above everyone else, and only Gwenn's clear voice could be heard in discordant complaint.

"Such a to-do," Gwenn said, smiling superciliously at Tippy who had been enthroned on a damask sofa. "Isn't it silly?"

"You're just jealous," Alice informed her, perching on the sofa arm, "because you eloped and missed all this. It's fun."

Gwenn shrugged and turned away, annoyed because even her husband had forgotten his role and was being one of the boys. He was perfectly absurd, she thought, behaving no better than little Davy or any of the smaller ones. Imitating the way Peter had looked when Tippy came down the aisle! Holding hands with young Donny and trying to shove a ring on his finger!

She sat a little to one side, wearing the most expensive dress in the room and scowling at the hilarity going on around her. Even Jenifer was joining in the fun, and Cyril. Lord and Lady Carlton were a couple of fools, she thought morosely. They had no dignity at all.

She watched Tippy jump up to defend the picture of herself, winking. Tippy declared she had been winking at her mother, not at Jonathan, and a concert of boo's answered her. The newspaper was needed for proof; and Gwenn, who had been sitting on it, had to pull it out and give it to Bitsy.

She wondered if pretty little Bitsy knew how lucky she was to live in a castle and to have met the young Queen of England. She doubted it; for Jenifer never had had any sense about rank or its privileges, not even in the army. She was too simple. She had trained the younger Jordons to be honest little characters, and it was no wonder they had all grown up with no ambition. I, she told herself, am different. If I had half a chance, I could make them fawn on me the way they do on Penny. If Bill would promote me the way Josh does her, I could show them all a thing or two.

Carrol was crossing the room, her arm around Davy's shoulder and holding the little Lang by the hand. The beautiful mother, Gwenn thought crossly. The saccharinely sweet, rich little mother.

"It's wonderful to be together, isn't it?" Carrol said, not particularly wanting to talk to Gwenn, but having sensed she needed attention. "That's a lovely dress you're wearing."

"Thank you. Garstain made it."

Gwenn smoothed the off-white satin sheath that encased her, feeling pity for the others who wore their skirts too full, while Carrol wondered how on earth they would steer her through an evening without a jealous tantrum.

The chatter was still going on, with the drawing room resembling a stage set, the leading actors in the middle, the supporting cast doing most of the work and carrying the scene; and in spite of her anxiety over Gwenn, Carrol had to watch. Tippy, as the leading lady, was struck dumb. She could only smack the newspaper with her fist and look pleadingly at her mother. Even the leading man was laughing at her.

"She really did wink at me," Mrs. Parrish finally called out like a prompter in the wings. "And I winked back."

"Oh, thank you, thank you!" Tippy cried, and rushed across the room to fall on her with grateful kisses. "My reputation was at stake and you saved it."

"By perjury," Jonathan shouted. "Mrs. Parrish, you destroyed the biggest moment of my life."

"The *what?*" Alice pushed into the vacant spot Tippy had left and declared, "Well, I like that. I'm practically a bride myself, and this is the way you treat me. Daddy, you'll have to take me back to Turkey with you."

The merriment continued; and under cover of it, Tippy leaned close to her mother and whispered, "Peter and I have a surprise for you. We can't tell you what it is, but don't feel bad if I don't pay much attention to you and Dad this evening. We'll be right with you till it's time for the boat to sail." She stopped, clapped her hand over her mouth, and exclaimed, "Oh, my soul, I didn't mean to say that! Just forget it. What I meant to tell you was. . . ."

"Your room's all ready," Mrs. Parrish answered, smiling happily. "Trudy bet me a cookie you'd be back."

"But it was Peter's idea. He gets the credit," Tippy said proudly. "Oh, Mums, he's so wonderful. He thinks of everything—even to giving me five dollars. I never thought I'd like taking money from a man, but it's thrilling, taking it from Peter. I'll spend it on a present for him."

She turned back to spring into her place on the stage again, but Perkins paused beside her. "Mrs. Jordon," he said in his correct voice that had awed her as a child, "Mrs. Parrish asks that you go in to dinner now."

"Thank you, Perkins. I knew," she said, hoping her mother couldn't hear, "that you were speaking to me, because I was the only one near you. Next time, try it when I'm walking around."

"Certainly, Mrs. Jordon." He hid a smile and returned gravely, "I'll attempt it after dinner."

She and Peter led the way into the dining room where the long table was stretched to its full length. The small children were to have a noisy meal in an adjoining breakfast room, so twenty people slid into their chairs and went on talking.

General Jordon hur-humphed at intervals during the meal, looking as if he were about to impart something of great importance, but when heads turned to look at him expectantly and conversation waited, he always subsided. "Carry on, carry on," he would boom. And it wasn't until the last of the ice cream and cake had disappeared and chairs were being pushed back that he stood beside Peter, and invited portentously, "Son, will you bring my new daughter and step into the library for a moment?"

"Sure, Dad." Peter moved Tippy's chair back and took her hand. "Goodness only knows what this may be," he said to her, as they followed the military back into a book-walled room with comfortable leather chairs.

"Sit down, sit down," the General rumbled. "And you, too, Dave. Come on in. This is as much your affair as mine."

Colonel Parrish leaned against the mantel and took out his cigarettes. "Oh, I don't think so," he said, offering the pack to Peter, astride the arm of Tippy's chair.

Tippy looked from one older man to the other. The big one was her father, too, she suddenly discovered to her surprise, and promptly began wondering what she should call him. Father? Dad? Or "Daddy," as Alcie did? But he was making his hur-humping noises again, and before she could decide which it should be, he began to speak.

"I doubt if you kids know," he said, "that junior officers and their wives haven't much rank on a transport. The wives have to share a cabin with other wives, and captains and lieutenants are bunked in together." He paused and looked out at them from under his heavy brows.

"We didn't know it, sir," Peter answered. "We haven't given it much thought, up to now."

"That's the way it is." He gave them time to stare unhappily at each other before he announced triumphantly, "But you won't have to worry. Two old campaigners with a little rank have worked a deal."

"You mean you have," Colonel Parrish put in. "Take the credit for it, P. J. You're still in the army and have some pull— I'm retired."

"Well, we worked it. You kids will have a cabin together. Inside of course," he hurried to say, lest they have grand ideas of a bridal suite. "Small, not choice—but you have it."

"Gosh, Dad, that's swell." Peter stood up to give this welcome gift its due, but his father stopped him by saying:

"Now just a minute. You're not to spread it around and brag. The ship isn't carrying its full complement and you're the only bride and groom, so that's how we got it for you. Take it easy. A lot of other young couples may feel resentful."

"We won't talk about it, Gen . . . Fa . . . I mean, Daddy," Tippy answered, floundering for a title and looking toward her own father whom she knew so much better and loved so much. "We can't ever tell you both how grateful we are."

"And there's one more little matter." General Jordon had come nobly through the scene which involved both him and his conspirator, but he almost burst his throat trying to clear the way for his next words to come out. "I want you kids to buy some furniture," he said. "This little check. . . ."

"No, Dad." Peter strode over and laid his arm across his father's shoulders. "I've saved up for that."

"And so have I. Living in Turkey doesn't cost me much."

"But a girl's boarding school and a military academy for two cost plenty. Hunhuh. Thanks, Dad, but no."

Peter was as tall as his father. Tippy watched the two, and something told her this was their moment together, just as she would have a secret time with her parents later. So she sat quite still, feeling love for blustery General Jordon steal into her heart.

"Take it, son," he said, "and make me happy. This is what your mother would want you to do, if she could be here. It would make her very happy, too."

Peter looked down at the check his father held out. "Not a thousand dollars, Dad. Make it five hundred."

"Take it, boy."

The check changed hands, and Peter folded it carefully. He stood with it pressed between his thumb and forefinger, unable to speak, until Tippy knew it was time to go over and hug them both.

"We'll buy beautiful furniture, Daddy," she said, kissing him. "And you'll come down to visit us, won't you?"

"Sometime." He looked at her with his great head close to hers and said in a gruffly tender voice she had never heard him use before, "Thank you for what you did for my Susan. It showed me that she's growing up; and it may make you feel better to know I'm planning on having her with me next year as my official little hostess."

"I'm awfully glad."

"Then let's go back and join the others. Dave," he marched across to say, "we have fine children."

"The best."

Colonel Parrish left the fireplace and the two men shook hands. They re-cemented a friendship that had been long and durable; and General Jordon, watching Tippy tuck the check in Peter's pocket with a look so tender that it bothered his throat, hur-humphed again and boomed, "Let's go in and join the others."

CHAPTER VII

"I could *push* the car faster than you're driving," Tippy grumbled, giving Bobby a look that should have withered him. "Do you expect to make the pier by noon?"

"Hope to." He slowed for a curve and an oncoming truck, and asked his father across her, "It isn't nine o'clock yet, is it?"

"No, and we haven't far to go now," Colonel Parrish answered.

Tippy was on her way to the ship. Peter was already there. The message that had taken him off ahead of her had come the night before, while the party at Gladstone was still in a talkative stage, and it had come from Trudy.

"A lieutenant colonel called you up," Trudy had told him over the telephone. "Seems like an officer who was to do some-tin' about the troops goin' aboard was taken to the hospital with appendicitis, and you're to come right away. You're to go straight to the transport and report to Colonel Robbins, in command of troops, or, if you can't locate him, to a Lieutenant Colonel Hall."

Trudy knew her army and had always given Colonel Parrish his messages with a minimum of words, concisely and with no gaps to be imagined or filled in, so she repeated carefully: "Colonel Robbins or Colonel Hall, on the transport, *General Blaine,* pier twenty-one, Brooklyn Army Base, as soon as you can."

That had started a real commotion. Bobby rushed out to bring Peter's uniform in from the car, and Tippy hindered more than she helped. "Oh, dear me," she cried excitedly, in the large mirrored powder room where Peter was changing from civilian clothes to the olive drab that was more familiar to him. "I don't see why I can't ride in with you and Bobby."

"Because—that's the wrong tie, honey, it's the one I just took off—because you'd have to turn around and come right back. Bobby's going to put Dad on the midnight train for Washington, and it would make you too late getting home." He knotted an o.d. tie under the collar of his khaki shirt, from practice and without looking in a mirror, and slid into his blouse. "Where's my cap?"

Tippy threw civilian garments about while she hunted the cap, and when she found it under his white shirt, she set it on his head and said proudly, "I feel so important, having you go off to work this way. I feel so *married.*"

"Umhum. It's a good thing I'm not leaving you alone at the Waldorf." Peter ran quick fingers over the insignia on his blouse to check them, the silver bars on his shoulders, the small gold tank on one lapel, the bright U.S. on the other. "All set," he said. "See you in the morning, darling."

And away he went, leaving Tippy to go home alone with her parents. She had slept in her own room; had risen to close her window before a tired, discouraged-looking dawn could make up its mind whether to get up with her or sleep an hour or two longer, and had rushed the family through breakfast so fast that Trudy, sitting on the back seat beside Mrs. Parrish, leaned over now to whisper, "I guess we won't have to worry about shovin' her up the gangway this time. She'll skitter up all by herself, alookin' for Mr. Peter."

Mrs. Parrish smiled and nodded as she moved her feet to make more room for Switzy. The two dogs had been almost friends that morning. Any sort of suitcase presaged trouble to Switzy, for Tippy always packed her clothes in one, then went away and left him, so he had huddled closer to Rollo, who took family departures in his stride and always held high hopes of being invited along.

They had sat by the door together; Rollo on guard and ready to frisk out at a sign, Switzy miserable and puzzled. They wore fine new collars; and whenever the red one on Switzy pushed too close to the green one beside it, a rumbling growl sent it quickly away again. "You didn't like me once," Rollo's growl said, "so don't bother me now. I may be leaving."

He sat up straight on his stubby legs, and all the time and energy a veterinarian had spent on him, plucking, washing, brushing, was wasted. He was just as frowzy as ever. Switzy was beautiful, but he was cold. His little shaved body had bare spots of skin showing here and there and the fluffy wool on his legs and topknot made fancy trimming but were in the wrong places for warmth. He shivered as silently and as inconspicuously as he could, but he bounced up with a yelp of joy when Tippy ran into the hall with one of her old sweaters.

"I can't think what we did with your new overcoat," she muttered, stuffing his front legs into the yellow sweater sleeves and tying a wide blue ribbon around his middle to hold him inside the makeshift suit. "I've looked everywhere but I can't find it. Stand still."

He was going. Even in this terrible costume, he was going somewhere; and he stumped awkwardly down the steps beside her, tripping over the long yellow sleeves and landing headlong in the car beside Rollo.

"Poor little Switzy," Mrs. Parrish said as she moved her feet and bent down to push up the wool so he could see he still had paws, "I'll miss you."

They had reached the crowded city of Brooklyn. The Army Base loomed ahead of them, and beyond it, hidden by the gray block of buildings and shut off from the civilian world by a high wire fence, was the port. There ships waited to carry soldiers and cargo, tanks, planes, and guns, to all parts of the world.

Bobby pulled up at a well-guarded gate where Colonel Parrish showed his pass and gave Tippy's status to two M.P.'s who checked a long list of passengers and saluted.

"You may drive right into the shed, sir," one said, "but please move your car away from the loading zone. The buses from the Port of Embarkation are beginning to come in now."

"Thank you, Sergeant." Colonel Parrish returned another salute, nodded for Bobby to move on, and said, patting Tippy's knee, "You see, we made it after all, and too early. You can unkink now."

"Not yet." She shook her head. "I'm like a spring that's been wound up too tight," she said. "When I let go—after we sail, I hope—I'll fly apart with a zing. Poor Peter."

It was dark in the shed and Rollo stood up to put his paws on the door and see where they were. Switzy wanted to look out, too, but his peculiar coat wouldn't let him. He only knew he was traveling a long way over wooden planking. There was something familiar about it. He crouched closer to Mrs. Parrish's feet, and when the car finally stopped and Tippy lifted him out, he tried not to shake. He knew where he was. He had been in this place once before, when he had been shipped home to Tippy from Germany, and the memory had stayed as fresh in his mind as the doctor's office where she sometimes took him. There was the big square hole with a wooden bridge beyond it that led straight up to a great, gray monster. There was water under the bridge; he could smell the water, and he sat down to roll miserable eyes up at Tippy.

"It's all right, lamb," she said, kneeling before him. "It won't be like that other time. I'll be right there with you. You'll be with Rollo in the kennels and I'll come down to see you every day."

She started to take off his unbecoming sweater, then felt the trembling shivers that shook him. "I think I'd better leave it on," she decided, snapping his new red leash to his collar. "Hold them both, Trudy, while I go over to the desk and see if Dad needs me for anything."

She gave a pat to the phlegmatic Rollo who was enjoying the sights—including a yapping puppy in a crate—while he waited for Peter. Rollo knew he had only to wait like a well-trained private until someone with authority came along and marched him somewhere. He turned his head away from the trembling Switzy with disdain.

"All set now," Colonel Parrish said. "Peter has your berthing card and all the papers, so we can go aboard. The buses are coming with families now, so let's give them some room."

Tippy took her new leashes from Trudy and squared her shoulders. "I'm thankful Peter and I didn't have to travel across the country and stay out at Fort Hamilton until we sailed," she said, watching mothers helping tired children out of the first bus that had pulled up, and fathers in uniform carrying small baggage and trying to identify larger pieces as they were unloaded. "Do you think I'll see Peter this morning?"

"I have a feeling he's pretty busy," her father answered, giving her a gentle prod.

"And will Penny and the others know where to find us?"

"They have their passes and will look us up."

Tippy was holding back. She was making a great show of tying the belt on her red coat, and Trudy kept a watchful eye on her. "She's doin' lots better than last time," she said in a low tone to Mrs. Parrish, satisfied that no lecture would be needed, only a crisp reminder of duty. And she pretended to reach again for the leashes. "You want me to take the dogs for you?" she asked. "Or is you able to do it?"

Tippy snatched off Switzy's sweater and shortened her grasp on the red and green straps. "My goodness," she said with great determination, "you act as if I'm *helpless!*"

"You look kind of droopy. For a young lady who's goin' off on her honeymoon, you seem reluctant."

"Just watch me." Tippy gave a nod that unseated her new black hat. "Boys," she commanded, "march!" And she strode firmly up the gangway.

Once on the tilted walk, Switzy was in a great hurry to reach the end of it. He and Rollo plunged up on four sure feet, dragging Tippy in her high heels, shoulder bag swinging, as she clutched at the rail with her free hand and tried to step between crossbars, meant to keep people from slipping but succeeding only in tripping her up.

She reached the top with a rush, catapulted down a step, and landed in an active, orderly scene. The place seemed filled with navy officers. The navy runs America's Military Sea Transport Service now, and its blue-clad officers were on duty by the dozens. The army had vanished completely. So had Peter.

"I suppose you're looking for the kennels," a young ensign stepped up and said to her. "The easiest way to find it is to take the elevator up to the lounge, walk straight through and along a corridor, and down an outside ladder—stairway to you. Hi, pooches," he said to the two upturned faces, one intent, the other without eyes or even any face at all. "Cute pups. My wife has one on board, a dachshund." And he explained quickly, "I'm not one of the official gang here. I just came down to see what's going on. Want me to show you the way?"

"We'll find it, thanks." Tippy took a firmer grip on her leashes and added, "I have to find my husband, too." She liked the sound of the words and was proud of the offhand way she had said them, so she tried them again. "My husband came aboard last night," she said. "Perhaps we'll see you and your wife this evening."

"Hope so. Straight through the lounge and down."

Bobby appeared beside her, bearing the large cardboard box with her wedding dress in it. "You left this in the car," he said.

A wisp of white tulle stuck out and she tried to shove it under the lid. She could feel a hot flush rising from her neck and smearing across her face, as red as her coat. "Get rid of it," she said in a desperate voice. "Take it away."

She felt as if the whole navy had stopped work to stare at her. What would they think of a bride lugging her wedding gown aboard? Actually, only one lieutenant commander had looked up from his charts to say to her father, "Mrs. Jordon is in cabin three-one-six, on boat deck. She'll find her baggage there." Perhaps, she thought hopefully, men didn't know the meaning of white tulle when they saw it. Nevertheless, she dragged her dogs to a more isolated spot.

Bobby and his box became part of a parade. He hated it as much as Tippy did; and once inside an elevator, he set the box on the floor and would have no more of it. "I don't care what becomes of it," he said, stalking out when the car stopped at the promenade deck, and walking into a large room equipped with leather chairs and divans, blond tables with lighted lamps on them. "I'll sit right here till it's time to go ashore."

The big room was almost empty. A few couples sat expectantly waiting or stood at the windows, looking across the glass-enclosed decks at the gray building they were tied to on one side, at The Narrows and Staten Island on the other. Mrs. Parrish and Trudy, knowing nothing else to do, sat down beside him.

It was a long time before Tippy and her father came back, before Tippy said, "The boys are comfortable. They're in a big cage together. Now what do we do?"

"We can look at your cabin, I suppose," her mother suggested.

It was a queer way for a bride to start on a honeymoon, Tippy thought dolefully; with just a family exclaiming delightedly over a small room that had double-decker beds against one wall, a red leather built-in couch along the other, two red chairs, two clothes closets, and a small tiled bathroom with a shower.

"Why it's lovely," Mrs. Parrish said, glad to see it so complete, and remembering an uncomfortable trip she had made on a transport. "I knew the services had taken this ship over from a commercial line, but I didn't know it was so beautiful. It seems to me I did hear they took out the swimming pool to make more troop space, but they left in air conditioning."

"Brrrr," Bobby shivered.

Peter's military brushes were on top of the built-in chest of drawers and his key case and a carton of cigarettes lay on the bottom bed, evidence of his really having been there, and Tippy wanted to touch something of his. It would be almost like holding onto Peter himself; so she edged over until she could pick up the key case and hold it clamped tightly in her fist.

If only he would come! She listened to her mother say how darling the room was; and later she listened to the Mac-Donalds, the Carltons, the younger Parrishes say the same thing. They liked the ship, squatting on the water like a long, gray bird, and they repeatedly told her how lucky she was to be taking a Southern cruise in such cold weather. There was still no sign of Peter. Loneliness welled up in Tippy's chest.

"Mums," she said, tagging along wherever the tour went, "I don't feel as if I can bear it when you leave. I don't think I can go so far away."

"Of course you can, lamb," Mrs. Parrish answered lightly, lonely and already bereft herself. "You'll have a wonderful time. Think of all the interesting letters you can write us."

"I'll write every day." Tippy gulped and clung to her mother's arm. "Does it cost much to telephone from down there?" she asked.

"I wouldn't know, dear, but don't do it. Be happy." Mrs. Parrish managed to move them both nearer the row of windows along the deck where Trudy was holding up first Lang and then little Joshu, so they could watch the band playing on the dock. "She's beginning to slip," she said to Trudy with a weak smile that meant, "and so am I."

"Nonsense." Trudy turned back briskly and left the two little boys to stand on tiptoe and see as much as they could. "Shame on you, Tippy Parrish," she scolded. "The idea of you lookin' so wilted, just because Mr. Peter ain't here to be with you." A brusque voice spoke through the public address system, commanding with authority, "All ashore that's going ashore";

and she warned quickly, "You'll have to put on a smile now, child, or you'll have your mama and papa worryin' about you. I know you'se a little lonesome now but it ain't goin' to last."

"All ashore that's going ashore," blared the voice again, just as Peter pushed open the heavy door from inside, and Tippy flew along the deck to meet him.

It didn't matter to her now if the people crowding the windows, taking a last glimpse of American shores or telling their relatives good-by, discovered she was a bride. She would have put on her wedding veil or worn a placard to show them Peter was hers again, and she flung herself against him.

"I almost didn't make it," he said above her head. "A cadre from St. Louis didn't show up and I've been checking with their headquarters."

"Find 'em yet?" Colonel Parrish asked, his interest in the army flaring up.

"They're aboard. It took a special bus to pick them up at Grand Central, with the captain of the ship telling us he'd sail on time, no matter what." He looked down and said, "I'm sorry, darling. I've been so worried about you."

"You needn't have been. But if you hadn't come just when you did, I might have followed the family ashore and got left behind." She could say that and laugh now, for the homesick lump was melting away. She could even tell each one of her relatives good-by without crying.

"We won't stay until you sail," Mrs. Parrish said to the relief of all of them. "There's nothing harder than standing outside, waving and calling to people who can't hear you, whether it's through a train window or on a dock. Just be happy, baby, and remember how happy we are for you."

"I will." Peter was standing close to her, and she gave out

messages and smiles. "Call up Alcie and tell her about our nice room," she urged Jenifer. "Gwenn won't care, but Alcie will. And we'll write you all postcards from the places where we stop." To Susan she said, "Don't forget you're coming down to visit us next summer."

"Oh, I won't. I'll think about it all the time." Susan's face glowed and she said shyly, "You've been so wonderful to me."

Tippy saved her mother and father until last. The lump came back in her throat when she clung to them. They were so brightly gay about it all. They seemed truly happy to have her go so far away, for they smiled as they hugged her. Laughter lines fanned out from her father's eyes and her mother's dimples went on a rampage. Tippy's face was a little grim, but she managed.

She made it last as long as she could by extracting promises of long letters, thinking up errands for things she had forgotten, urging them to take good care of themselves; but at last they had to follow the others down a broad stairway that led far, far below, to the deck where the gangway was. Tippy stood at the top, watching them go around the landings, and waving gallantly.

They were gone. Even by leaning over the railing she could no longer see the tops of their heads, and she cried to Peter, "Oh, let's have one last look at them!" And they raced back to the windows on the deck.

The ship's horn gave a long throaty blast. Sailors stood by to pull away the bridge between the ship and the shore, a naval officer raced aboard with last dispatches, the band played louder. Tippy knew one waving hand would be lost among all the others that fluttered, but she waved it anyway. She watched her father take her mother's arm when they reached the dock and bend his head to hear something she was saying. The tender gesture was too much. Her set smile faded and the tears came.

"There, there, darling," Peter soothed; and let her cry against his chest.

CHAPTER VIII

TIPPY's smile came back again the moment the ship's engines began to revolve and throb in earnest. She was on her way. A wide gulf of water separated her from her past, and a long lane of ocean, miles and miles of it, led to her future. She knew she couldn't have both. She couldn't turn the ship around and still go to Panama with Peter, so she danced about the small room while she and Peter unpacked, hanging their clothes neatly in the closets at first, then, as the ship began to roll and pitch, making stabs at the rods and holding on.

The sea was rough. Rain and sleet began to beat down, splattering the decks and portholes like bullets, and the wind blew giant waves into hurdles. They made high, crooked barriers that the Military Transport *Blaine* took with valiant sprightliness, lifting more than three hundred cabin-class passengers and fifteen hundred troops up with it, then pitching them down again in a lunging roll that turned three-fourths of them a sickly green.

Tippy loved it. She lurched from the closet to the dresser with snatches at a chair on her way; and by the time the ship had flung itself around Sandy Hook and was headed South, she and Peter had the little cabin, what she called, "shipshape."

It was to be their home for the next eleven days and it already had a lived-in look: a pile of the latest magazines lay on the end of the long, red sofa; a small traveling clock ticked away on top of the high chest beside a *bon voyage* basket that had roses sprouting like a fountain from a mound of fruit. There was nothing more to do, so she brushed her black wool dress and put on fresh lipstick in the tiny bathroom, then she and Peter closed their first front door and went plunging and swaying down a flight of stairs to the lounge.

"To use nautical terms," Peter said when they reached bottom safely, "we clung to the bulkhead, not the wall, and descended the ladder."

"Descended, my eye," she retorted, planting her feet in a wide foyer and hoping she could steer a course through a doorway, to a circle of chairs she saw beyond. "We practically *fell* down."

He linked their arms together for safety, and together they negotiated it over a high sill and paused for balance again. "Let's roll over there by the windows," he suggested, as the ship turned on its side and headed them in the right direction.

They were almost there when a voice shouted, "Pete Jordon, by all that's living!" and Tippy recognized the young ensign who had told her where to find the kennels. He came rolling toward them with his hand outstretched, and asking, "Remember me? Al Blake? Class of 51, Annapolis?"

"I sure do." Peter let go of Tippy and the two hands met and began to pump.

"I never expected to see the old Gray Terror himself," Al Blake cried, giving Peter's back a thump but hanging on to turn and call, "Molly, come over here and meet the greatest halfback West Point ever turned out. Hey, you Gwynns and Staglianos, come along, too. Well, what do you know!"

Five people managed to skirt a little boy who was being very sick on the waxed floor. Four of them arrived, but the fifth, a young marine lieutenant, turned back and made for the outside deck and fresh air.

"Imagine a marine not being able to take it," Al jeered, introducing the others. "Kathy and Miles Stagliano," he said, "Connie Gwynn, she's the sturdier half of the Gwynns, and this is Molly. The Jordons," he explained to his wife, "have two dogs in the kennels, and you're shaking hands with a guy who was all-American for three years straight. He made a sucker out of me every time I played against him, and, boy, was Navy glad when he graduated. Say, let's all sit down."

He was so likeable, extolling Peter's prowess. Nothing could stop him. Peter tried, but Ensign Blake was patently a hero worshiper; and he sat on the arm of Molly's chair, showing how stupid he had looked when Peter side-stepped his flying tackle and ran for a touchdown.

Tippy looked at Molly and winked. She liked her. Snub-nosed, wide-mouthed, with a poodle haircut, she rested her chin on her husband's knee and asked across him, "Where are you going to be stationed?"

"In Panama. On the Pacific side, at Fort Clayton. Where are you?"

"Al has his first shore duty since we've been married." Molly confided, with shining black eyes. "We're to be at Amador. It's on the Pacific side, too, so we won't be very far apart. Oh, grand! Kathey and Miles are getting off at Guantánamo, and the Gwynns at Trinidad."

Tippy turned to the other girls. They were attractive, quiet blondes, and she learned that the Gwynns had a small baby, quite happily asleep in his crib, and the Staglianos hoped to

WELCOME HOME, MRS. JORDON

have one by Easter. Of the three she was glad it was to be the vivacious Molly living near her.

The group sat and talked until a little Filipino came through, playing mess call on his chimes, and the public address system announced the second sitting for lunch.

"The elevator only runs when it feels like it," Peter said, from having lived on the ship the night before. "We'd better take the stairs." So they all plunged down.

The sea continued its pranks for three days. Tippy never knew when Peter might disappear in his working uniform—shirt and slacks and tanker's boots—and be gone for hours at a time. He was in charge of a soldiers' troop compartment; and since Al had one for the navy, she and Molly spent a great deal of time together. They climbed carefully down to the kennels each morning, played canasta in the afternoon, and hopefully saved two seats between them at the movies in the evening.

And then, like a child that tires of being naughty, the sea turned calm and sunny. Flying fish skimmed over the blue water, heavy clothes were packed away and out came cotton dresses, khaki uniforms, and sun suits and shorts for the great open sun deck.

The promenade was deserted. Steamer chairs and shuffleboard in the sun were in vogue, and the small post exchange sold countless bottles of sun-tan oil and soothing lotions. Passengers were either red and peeling or tanning a beautiful brown by the time they reached Cuba and sailed into the beautiful harbor at Guantánamo.

"Peter," Tippy cried breathlessly, finding him looking over the starboard rail, just below the captain's bridge, and poking him with the new white purse that had been in her Christmas box, "they're going to let us off the ship! We're to be taken around to see the sights in a bus, and I've been hunting on every deck for you. A colonel told me about it."

"Swell. That means we can tell the Staglianos good-by on shore."

"And we're to visit all the post exchanges—three of them, air force, marine, and navy—and they have just about everything in them, the colonel said. And we can lunch at the club. Do you suppose," she calmed down enough to ask, "we can take the boys off, too?"

"Not a chance. That much I know." Peter pulled her in beside him at the rail, to show her a sign painted on a long shed they were gliding past. It said "WELCOME TO GUANTANAMO," and a band played beneath it. Women in full cotton skirts, bare-legged and hatless, held onto small children and waved at the ship, while men in khaki, tieless, some even in khaki shorts, stood about in groups. "Gosh, it's exciting," he said. "It's kind of like a cruise, isn't it?"

It became even more like a cruise as the days went on. There was San Juan, in Puerto Rico with the "lady mayor" coming out in her red fire boat to welcome the transport, little boys diving for coins, a very sumptuous lunch at the big Caribe Hilton Hotel, and tourist shops to visit. There was Port-of-Spain in Trinidad, with sightseeing and lunch on a mountain, and more shops. Tippy bought a large basket and filled it with purchases: a bowl from Guantánamo, made of native mahogany, a straw purse that had come from Haiti, cigarette boxes and ashtrays, a silver bracelet she had watched an artisan make in Trinidad; and she and Peter each had a bright blue shirt with little lions woven into them. She even had a full, gathered skirt to match hers.

"I've just loved going ashore with you and coming back to our boat again, she said on their last night, with a wistful little sigh, sitting in a steamer chair on the open sun deck beside Peter, under a starry sky and listening to the swish, swish of waves. "Tomorrow, it will all be over. Oh, I wish we could go on and on."

"And miss having our house?" He lifted her hand from the chair to hold it in his. "This is only the beginning, Tip," he said. "Tomorrow's when our real life will start. Think how swell it's going to be, with everything all shining new."

"I know it. I'm excited and trembly about that, wondering how our house will look, who our neighbors will be, and how well I'll be able to manage. I'm really so trembly," she said, "that I try not think about it. My heart bumps and thumps so hard that I just try to keep my mind on what I'm doing today. I won't let myself look ahead. Molly feels sort of the same way," she explained seriously. "She's only been married a year and has never had a house of her own before or been very far away from her family. So we pretend we're only on a trip; and when we do plan, we decide to call each other up every fifteen minutes to find out how the other one's coming along. Just in the daytime, that is. I'll have you with me at night."

"I'll come home and say, 'Gee whizz, Mrs. Jordon, you've certainly done wonders with this dump.' It may be a dump," he reminded. "I'm not very high-ranking, you know."

"Mums said her first house was. It was so old it had rats and roaches, and splinters in the floor. They didn't dare let David crawl around, and they burned soft coal, even in a cookstove. She said the way I'm starting out is very plush, compared to the old days, and the military part of Panama can't be *very* old."

"How about Termite Row that somebody told us about? We might live there, and they said it didn't get its nickname for nothing."

"We'd like it. But the captain we met—you know, the one

who's been in the States on leave and said some friends of his might sell us their grass rugs? He thinks we'll probably get his friend's house in Four Hundred Area, since you're taking over his job."

"Let's hope so."

Two shadows appeared at the top of the aft ladder and came along the deck. Peter relinquished Tippy's hand reluctantly and got up to drag two more chairs nearer theirs. He liked Al and Molly, but he liked these quiet talks with Tippy better. "Oh, well," he said, bending down and knowing she would understand what he meant, "we'll have hundreds and hundreds of starry nights."

"Our very special-to-order ones." She reached up to touch his cheek, and called out, "Has the dancing started, Molly?"

"Not yet. The movie's just over and the lounge is full of kids. Our Hawaiian table steward is going to play the electric zither thing, so we told him we'd come back. Thanks, Peter." Molly swung herself into the deck chair and leaned back. "I'd rather dance up here on the shuffleboard court," she said.

"They'll pipe the music up." Peter found Tippy's hand again as a late yellow moon rose out of the sea to blind the stars. "Ummm," he said, "I think life in the Tropics is going to suit me fine."

The moon rose higher and higher in its course across the sky; soft music floated over the deck, and strolling couples climbed the ladder to breathe the soft, salty air and stayed to dance. It seemed only a little while until they heard *Aloha*, played with haunting sweetness by the little band of Hawaiian musicians who served faithfully as stewards during the day.

"Good-night, all," Peter called along the companionway, down on boat deck again and holding open their cabin door for Tippy. "See you at early breakfast."

The little room was quite bare. Luggage was gone. Piled in a mound on a lower deck, it was just anybody's luggage now, tagged and stacked; and the little cotton suit Tippy took off had a whole closet to itself. A few toilet articles and the traveling clock were the only objects to make them know the cabin was still theirs.

"Nice little room," she said, sitting on the red sofa to survey it." It's been so good to us. We're the first people it's ever held, and I do hope other couples will love it and take as good care of it as we have. I'll tell it good-by before we leave and wish it good luck."

But when morning came there was no time. She had too many addresses to write down, so much to see from the top-most rail.

Fruit boats were tied in their docks. French ships, Swedish, British liners, all waited their turn to go through the locks and out into the vast Pacific Ocean. The blue harbor was a busier place than quiet San Juan, that had old El Moro standing guard on a cliff; busier even than Port-of-Spain, where cruise ships lay idly at anchor, and people from tiny, verdant islands off the shore sailed lazily about in the bay or trolled for fish in motor boats. Panama had an American look.

Buildings along the shore were shining white and administrative. They had been built for efficiency and economy of effort and time, and they looked as if they defied the populace to shirk its duty or loiter under the hot Panamanian sun. Even the big transport followed their example and headed for her slip without stirring the water unnecessarily, gliding silently along the dock, her engines still.

Tippy watched the mooring lines go out, and thought, Whatever it's going to be like—I'm home.

CHAPTER IX

ALTHOUGH Tippy had confessed that she was timid about facing her future, Peter watched her go down the gangway ahead of him at Colón, and thought she marched down as if she were going into battle. Sailors slouched along under their sea bags, soldiers bore their duffel bags on sagging shoulders, but Tippy's little back was militantly straight. Not even the two dogs scrambling toward freedom or her basket of souvenirs could throw her off her stride. She went with her head high, and keeping time to the welcoming band.

It was lucky for his peace of mind that he was behind her, not where he could see the expression on her face. It was a look of grim determination. She stared straight ahead, at the people on the dock, at the fenced-in area where her smaller baggage waited, at a giant crane that swung trunks over the water and deposited them in a herd, like waiting cattle. She was afraid to look back at the ship, the dear ship that would be homeward bound in a day or two. She was afraid even to speak to the plunging dogs, lest her voice break with a homesickness that was far worse than the stomach upsets the other passengers were free from, now that their feet were on land. The ache in Tippy's heart was just beginning again.

She reached the wide, worn boards of solid footing and the two little dogs danced in wild circles around her. Peter was so busy. He found a Panamanian porter with a hand truck and loaded their belongings on it; he found an officer who told him where he could pick up his car as soon as it was unloaded, where to fill out necessary papers, and what he must do to obtain a new license for it. By the time he was able to find Tippy again in the crowd, she was watching soldiers and military families being put aboard a train for the trip across the Isthmus, and had control of herself again.

"Don't bother about us," she said quickly, as he charged up to her, a sheaf of papers in his hand. "Just forget us. Do the things you have to do and we'll walk around outside." That was the way her mother had always talked; and even though she wanted to hang on to the hem of Peter's light tropical worsted blouse, she gave him the competent army wife smile her mother had always used. "I'll walk the boys," she said.

"O.K. That officer I was talking to said the shops are right over on Front Street, and there's a Navy Club where you can have some lunch if I don't finish up before then. Suppose I meet you there."

"All right."

They began walking along together through the open but airless shed that was filled with buses and the waiting train, their porter trundling their luggage ahead of them; and Tippy said chattily, "Molly and Al drove off with some friends who met them. They won't have their car until the next boat. I'm glad we have ours, though. It's so much nicer to start out alone."

"By late afternoon we should be in our house—if we have one," he stopped to say. "Here, honey, let me carry that coat. Are you as hot as I am?"

Tippy looked cool in her aqua cotton suit, but she nodded.

"I'm melting," she confessed, as Peter laid her coat over the one he carried and took her basket of treasures from her. "Do you suppose it's always this hot down here?" she asked.

"I guess so. I heard a woman tell a couple of complaining arrivals that this is actually a nice, cool day. She even held out the hope that after a couple of weeks your feet stop swelling and you get used to the humidity. Happy thought."

She glanced up quickly to see if he were disappointed or doubtful, as she was. He looked happy. He looked as if he were about to whistle or burst into song; and she felt ashamed of the silly lump that, no matter how hard she pretended, would stay lodged somewhere in her middle, so gave a little skip that was supposed to show a suppressed excitement, comparable to his.

A plot of palm trees came into view, white cement and a sweltering sun. Peter and his Panamanian baggageman would soon turn off to the left and she would head for the little green park that looked like an oasis to her. "Don't worry," she said. "I know where you're to meet us, and can keep on asking people till I find the place."

There was no chance to wait for his reply. Switzy jerked the leashes from her hand and took off at a gallop, with Rollo paddling along behind him as fast as his short legs would go. "Wait!" she screamed, and ran panting after them, snatching at the straps just out of her reach, and stopping on a curb to squeeze shut her eyes when they dashed across a street in the path of a car.

They were headed for the park which formed a wide center strip between two lanes of traffic on Front Street, and when they reached it safely, she sank down on a bench under a palm tree and thankfully watched them tear up and down on the brownish, green grass.

"Oh, you foolish boys," she scolded, when they came back to her. "Don't you know you might have been killed? You might not have lived to go back to America again. Think of that! What if you'd never seen America again, or Mums and Dad? What if you couldn't ever have gone *home?*"

They didn't care. One place was as good as another to them, for home was where she was, and they flopped down and rolled about, squirming and rubbing the odor of the kennels into the ground.

Tippy sat with the loops on the ends of their leashes firmly hooked over her finger. A long row of shops stretched for blocks before her: china shops, silver shops, leather, straw, perfume, even Oriental antiques. A shady gallery covered their open fronts and gave them a cool and pleasant look; so when she had her breath back and the dogs had tired of lying with their feet kicking the air, she got up and walked them across the street.

She strolled aimlessly for a time, imagining all the gifts she would like to buy and take home to her family. She had quite an assortment by the time she reached a large department store and wandered in through its open door. It could have been a branch of Sears Roebuck or Montgomery Ward, and she wondered if it might be. Refrigerators, stoves, washing machines, and small electric appliances took up a great deal of floor space, and there were counters of scarves, jewelry, men's wear, even a bakery and grocery department. An elevator at the back constantly opened and closed its doors for hurrying Americans.

"Could you please tell me," she asked, going over to a counter to speak to a clerk, "the name of this store?"

"*Eet ees,*" a soft Spanish accent informed her, "the American

Commissary. Here you buy what you need: dresses, furniture, all you desire."

"Thank you."

Tippy thought it was a funny-looking commissary. It would send her mother straight to seventh heaven; and she hoped, and was almost sure, that someday it would affect her the same way. It would, when she and Peter came in together, but just now it was only another store to her and she was killing time. Switzy tugged at his leash so she moved on.

The Navy Club, when she finally reached it, was still another surprise. She had expected to seat herself in a dim, cool lounge where electric fans whirred pleasantly, but she walked straight from the street into a large, noisy cafeteria. Even a juke box played. Gum machines clanked, placards pointed to a beauty shop and a movie theater, and the place was crowded with tables and chairs.

"This is our last stop," she told her two patient escorts, standing in line for a sandwich and three paper cups of milk. "I'll take you outside to drink your lunch."

It was two hours later before she saw a familiar green club coupé hustling along the hot street. Rollo was taking a nap, but she yanked him up and snatched the extra sandwich and milk she had gone back to buy. "Here's your lunch," she cried, shoving them at Peter. She pushed the dogs over the back of the seat and herself into place, all in one swift gesture, as she asked, "Dear Gussie, where were you?"

"I had to go to the bank. It seems I needed a certified check for the license and all the mess of stickers on the windshield. Thanks for the food. And," he went on, munching, "our car hadn't come off till fourth. I left a bunch still waiting. Are you ready?"

"*Ready?*" she laughed. "I'm on my way. But Peter, I did find the most wonderful store!" And she prepared to describe the commissary to him.

"Um," he answered, looking at some road signs and trying to decide which way he should turn. "I guess this is right, but we have a Y coming up pretty soon so you'd better read the map." He poked a piece of paper at her, and they settled down to find their way across the Isthmus, to Panama City.

The road was long. The sky shone its sun on them with blistering heat, as if it wanted to see how quickly it could cook them; and when it had them sizzling to its satisfaction, it turned on a faucet and poured down water.

"This isn't rain," Tippy said, steaming inside the closed car. "It's a cloudburst. It's worse than a Turkish bath. Do you suppose it does this way all the time?"

"It couldn't," he answered, loosening his tie and mopping his forehead with a piece of her cleansing tissue. "Hasn't everyone told us this is the dry season? How can it rain in the *dry* season?"

"It's doing a wonderful job of showing me what it would be like if it should rain, then," she informed him. "Well, I wish you'd look."

As suddenly as it had vanished the sun came back. It brought a little breeze with it, and they leaned out to drink in the fresh air and look at one of the great locks. The man-made waterway had a freighter in it. It was lifting the ship one step farther on its journey, moving it along until another lock received it and lifted it even higher. In three hours it would glide out, free again, and in another ocean.

"It's exciting," Tippy said; and for the first time really knew that it was.

They passed little villages; just ordinary small clusters of houses, where people lived out their simple lives and children played in the dust. They passed a few beautiful homes, too, set in the hills with palm trees and flowering vines for decorations, and higher, rolling mountains for a backdrop. And at last they rolled over a long, winding hill and saw a lighthouse ahead of them.

"There she is!" Peter said, pointing. "A guy told me to watch for a lighthouse. He said it would be on the left side of the road, and a bridge—the Miraflores, I think he called it— would be on the right. He said that as soon as we see it . . . yep, that's it. That's good old Fort Clayton."

Tippy sat up to peer through the windshield. She saw yellow stuccoed buildings with wide porches surrounded by a high, wire fence. A main building had no porches. Its entrance was an impressive archway with gilded crossed sabers above it and the numerals 45 above them. "My goodness," she said, looking all along the row of barracks, "nothing has any windows."

"Huh?"

"I mean there isn't any glass in the windows. Just wide roofs above them so it can't rain in. And look. All those houses back on the hills—they haven't glass either. Won't we have glass windows?" she asked.

"I doubt it. Not if it's always this hot."

Peter turned the car through a gateway beside the lighthouse. There was a sentry box but no sentry, so he went on to park beneath the gold sabers. "I don't think this will take very long," he said. "I'll just have to report in. Gosh, where's my tie?"

"Right here." Tippy swung the rear view mirror around so he could look into it, and took his blouse from the back of the seat.

She knew he was nervous from the way he fumbled with

the Manila envelope and the copies of his orders in it; and she gave a little gasp when he finally stepped out and another flash of rain pelted down on him.

I'd be nervous, too, she thought, cranking up the windows again. I'd fall apart if I were reporting for a new job. Look how scared I am, just reporting to a new house. It may be a hateful house, but if I don't like it I can scout around the way Mums used to do and find us a better one when it's vacant. If Peter doesn't like his job, he's stuck. "Peter," she turned around to tell the quiet ones perched on cases on the back seat, "has a great deal of responsibility on his shoulders, so don't bother him any more than you can help. Until he shakes down in this new job it's up to us to do everything we can for him. We're all army, so let's remember that."

Switzy moved closer to Rollo, who was very patient with him. Rollo seemed to have developed a patient attitude on the journey, Switzy a resigned one, and they were stuck together like a couple of plasters. "Everything's going to be a lot of fun," Tippy told them cheerfully, and sincerely hoped it was.

Those were Peter's first words, in essence, when he came back. "The setup's swell," he said, climbing into the car and pitching his cap and tie to her again. "I met my immediate boss, Captain Taylor—'Red' to all his superiors, because he has red hair—and the lieutenant colonel in command of our outfit, Colonel Tillson. I met my major, too, but I couldn't quite understand his name. It's something like Blaisdell or Blaisdon, I don't know which."

"Were they nice?"

"Regular. Said they need me and had heard of my record at the Point, stuff like that. Colonel Tillson knows David and thinks he's met your father and mine. All the wives are coming to call on you—to give you pointers on things—and I have the key to our house."

"Oh, Peter, I'm so proud of you." She leaned over with him as he turned the ignition key, and said with their faces close together, "This is the first time I've really realized that you're a young officer reporting for duty. I've thought more about our living down here, what it would be like, and not very much about the fact that it's another step in your career. You're taking your first step toward becoming Commander in Chief of the Armies," she said proudly.

"My second," he laughed. "I took the first one when I went to Texas. Let's take the third toward home."

"Darn it, you're always so modest," Tippy criticized proudly. "I don't praise you enough; I never have. I always took for granted all the nice things you did for me, and I used to watch you gallop up and down the football field without ever really telling you how thrilled I was or bragging about you the way Al did. I *was* thrilled, Peter. I am, right now."

"I know it, childie. We're proud of each other."

"But I've been so selfish," she persisted. "Even this morning. I wanted to be with you but I wanted to turn around and go home, too. I wasn't very helpful."

"Helpful? Why, Tippy," he said in amazement, "what do you think it meant to me to have you say you'd look after yourself? Most wives would have hung around and hampered a guy or else had to be made comfortable first and seated somewhere. Gee, honey, I could tend to my business and not worry about you."

"I hadn't thought of it that way." She leaned back against the seat with a grateful sigh, but was up again to say quickly, "Now we're back to *me* again. Why can't we ever stay on the the subject of *you?*"

"Because we're one and the same. You're proud of me, I'm proud of you—let's go home."

"Can you find it?"

"I can darn well try. If we take a tour on the way, you won't mind, will you?"

"I'll look at everything as if I had a dozen eyes."

They wound along well-kept roads where green grass flourished on either side and flowers bloomed riotously. One long street had large houses facing a golf course. "Kings Row," Peter said, flipping his hand; then he grinned and added, "Captain Taylor told me. The top brass lives there. See their name plates under the top steps? All colonels. We may as well move on."

"Funny how high the houses are built up," Tippy said, looking. "They seem to be standing on stilts, and some of them have cars parked underneath and part of the space made into an outdoor room. See the tables and chairs under this one? And a regular laundry, and clotheslines."

"I guess, as hot as it is, people spend a lot of time under there." Peter turned along a section of double, gray frame houses, not so pretty as the colonels' quarters, and they decided it might be Termite Row. "It isn't our street I know," Peter said, "because our house is yellow."

"Then try that bunch over there," she pointed. "I see a lot of yellow houses way over beyond the movie theater. I wonder what that big green building is on the hill. It looks like a country club."

"Hospital. Let's stay away from there."

The car poked along between two rows of yellow houses, stuccoed the same as the soldiers' barracks, their red-tiled roofs overhanging their many windows like guarding brows. The houses seemed all windows. "Yep," Peter said with satisfaction, "we're gaining on it. These numbers are right. Do you see anything that looks empty and has 208 stenciled on the steps?"

"Stop! Right here. Oh, Peter, *stop!* This is ours!" she cried. "It has *Lieutenant Jordon* on it!"

"By gum, it has. And it has one of those open-room affairs underneath, too, and someone has left a wooden swing hanging in it. Gosh, it's a dandy, with all the grass and trees and flowers around it. What are all those red things called?"

"Hibiscus. And those are mimosa trees, and the vine climbing up is a bougainvillaea." Tippy was proud of her floral knowledge, and she hopped out of the car before it had quite stopped in the driveway to wave her arms and say, "And all the others are palms." The dogs almost knocked her down as they leaped for freedom, so she let them go barking and tearing over the lawn, their leashes flying out behind them.

She and Peter walked up a high flight of steps, and while he tried the new key in its lock, she stood looking up at the wide eaves above her. "We had a roof sort of like this in Bavaria," she said, "only not quite so broad because we had windows to close when it rained. It's going to seem awfully queer to hear everything our neighbors say." And she exclaimed at a sudden discovery, "Why, we haven't any screens!"

"No flies in Panama."

The new key turned as easily as it had for its previous tenants, and he pushed open the door before he reached down and scooped her up in his arms. "Welcome, my darling," he said before he kissed her and set her on her feet in a cool, tiled hall.

Tippy leaned against him for a moment while she turned her head and looked around her. A living room, all windows, opened on the left of the hall and turned a corner to make a dining ell. More windows were on her right, and two open doors at the back showed a kitchen and a small half bathroom.

The house was airy but compact, and a neat little stairway led upstairs to three bedrooms and another bath, but Peter and Tippy walked into their empty living room with its cool, green walls.

"Why, the floors are all tiled," Tippy exulted, looking down. "Isn't that nice? And there's the same old army dining-room furniture that we grew up with! Oh, it makes me feel so at home."

She ran into the ell to stroke the mahogany table and solid, wide-backed chairs, then hurried on to push open another door to the kitchen. "A stove. And an electric refrigerator," she breathed, with such glee that Peter wondered what she had expected to see in a kitchen. "And there are pans on the stove and food in the refrigerator. Come here and see!"

"The post always does that for people moving in down here, so they tell me." He stood behind her, looking at a beautiful bottle of milk, a carton of eggs, bacon, and a box of butter. "It's part of the welcome, which we pay for. Two cots are made up upstairs, and we'll be dunned for everything."

"I don't care. It's worth it, it's just so nice." Tippy closed the white porcelain door reluctantly. "I think I'd like to cook something," she said.

"Not tonight, you don't." He swung her around. "Mrs. Jordon," he asked, smiling down at her, "what would you say to shaking out that dreamy pink dress you brought and going in to El Panama to dinner, to dine and dance on the roof?"

"What would we do with the boys?"

"Feed 'em and leave 'em. They'll be all right."

"They'll be together, won't they? Just as you and I are. Of course they don't love each other the way we do, but they can talk. Oh, Peter," her eyes were like stars as she said, "You do think of the loveliest ways to keep me happy."

"And what would you say to spending the night there? It's a famously beautiful hotel and we saved some money by skipping one night at the Waldorf. I hear you really can see the sun come up over the Pacific from its rooms on the ocean side. I'd like to see it once, wouldn't you?"

"I don't believe it, but I'd love to."

"And we can come back and pick up the boys in the morning, then go out and buy our furniture. The major said for me to take three or four days to get settled."

"Were ever two people so lucky! I'm positively dizzy with happiness." She hugged him as hard as she could before she jerked his head down to kiss him. "Peter Jordon," she said softly, "it's no wonder I love you."

CHAPTER X

I⊤ was cool under the house, so Tippy sat in the wooden swing that had its chains fastened to joists under the dining-room floor. She wasn't swinging, for her knees were propped up to hold a yellow pad that matched her shorts, and she wrote busily. The dogs lay on the cool cement, and every now and then Rollo gave a rumbling growl to keep Switzy in his place.

Rollo had lost his patient look and had become a soldier's dog again, always present at retreat and joining the early evening guard on sentry duty; Switzy had changed from an arrogant little scrapper to a fawning dependent that tagged along behind, adoringly, but at a safe and wary distance.

"Quiet, boys," Tippy said, licking her pencil. "I'm busy."

She was making a list and a menu. The house was finished. There was nothing more she could do to it, for all the money was gone. Rattan furniture with rose cushions sprinkled the living room on thick grass rugs; she and Molly had made green drapes together and she had hung hers on cranes that let them swing away from the windows and not interfere with the breeze that came in through the slats of the louvers. Flower prints hung on the walls and wedding gifts were on glass-topped tables. Even two bedrooms were fluffy and cool with chintz, but the third was still unfurnished and held empty trunk lockers and the leftovers.

She had lived in the house a month, and now she was planning a party.

"Quiet, boys," she said automatically, although neither had made a sound. "I think this does it."

A horn tooted a short squawk in the driveway, and she sprang out of the swing with a bounce that rattled its chains. "Goodness, darling, I didn't hear you coming!" she cried, padding around the clothesline on flat, open sandals to meet Peter as he got out of the car. "Want to stay out here or go inside?" she asked, lifting her face for his kiss.

"I'm so grubby and hot I'd better wash up. Ummm, you smell like flowers," he said, sniffing her hair.

"It's the new perfume I bought at the P.X. Perfume's so cheap down here I'm having a field day. I keep hoping someone we know will go home to the States soon, so I can send Mums some without duty."

They walked around the front of the house and stopped in the hall as they always did to admire the beauty they had created. "It looks so cool," Peter said. "Somehow, you've managed to give it the warmth of looking lived in, yet coolness, too. You're a wonder, Mrs. Jordon."

"And you're the best picture hanger and curtain 'putter-upper' I know, Lieutenant. We did it together, darling. Run scrub off the dirt and hurry back."

Peter bounded up the stairs, forgetting how hot and tired he had been, while Tippy hummed a happy way to the kitchen.

She took ice cubes from a tray, slices of lemon from a dish, and dropped them into tall glasses. Then she poured tea from a pitcher and carried the glasses back to the living room. "Here you are," she said as Peter came back. "Quick work on both our parts."

His light hair was darkly damp from his shower and he wore

blue denim shorts and a thin, short-sleeved shirt. Leather sandals let his toes peep through, and he wriggled them comfortably when he was stretched out in his deep chair with an ottoman that they had chosen especially for him. "You spoil me just fine," he said, taking the glass. "What have you been doing all day?"

"Working on the house, and I wrote to Penny." A little cloud drifted into Tippy's eyes but vanished. The days were so long when she was alone in the house, but they sped by on wings when Peter came home. So she said quickly, to justify herself to herself for all the letters she wrote her family, "Penny didn't believe the sun really does come up over the Pacific, even though I told her it shone in our eyes the morning we woke up in the hotel and that we saw it rise right out of the ocean, so I sent her a piece of a map. She can see the way the land curves around and faces East. That ought to fix her. And, oh, yes, I had a caller."

"Who came this time?"

"Mrs. Bathurst. She's a colonel's wife and he's a big-shot engineer, or something." Tippy sat down in a cushioned rattan chair, too, and said with a puzzled expression, "You know, there must be something wrong with me."

"Why?"

"People treat me as if I haven't good sense. I gave Mrs. Bathurst iced tea this afternoon, and I did it very nicely, too, in our best crystal glasses and with little cookies on a Dresden plate, and she looked at me as if she were surprised I could do it. She even said, 'How beautifully you've arranged your quarters, for a bride.' And the other day when I was in our commissary, I saw two women watching me. One of them said to the other, just as if I was deaf, 'Sweet.'; and the other one answered, 'And so young.' Poodles," she declared. "I'm not young. I'm married."

Peter laughed and looked across at her. Late sunlight filtering in touched her golden curls and made her look like a good little angel. She did look much too young to have done such a bang-up decorating job, he thought, to bake cookies, clean, scour, yet always be as fresh as if she'd just stepped out of a shower.

But she was still protesting, "They don't know me. I suppose it's time to show them how really efficient I am."

"Such as?"

"Such as giving a party. We're indebted to dozens of couples on the post," she went on thoughtfully, stirring the lemon around and around in her glass. "Lots of people have entertained us, but I think I'll start out with a seated dinner and have just the rank."

"Shouldn't we get in a cook?"

"Of course not."

The subject of a cook had come up at regular intervals. Servants were cheap in Panama, Peter pointed out, and they might never be able to afford one again. He said Tippy worked too hard, and she argued, "But what would I do? I can't sit around all day. I'm happier when I'm working."

She knew she was. She didn't write so many letters when she had dusting to do and dishes to wash. Sometimes she wished she had more. She hunted up work to keep her mind busy, to stop worrying about her mother driving herself to market over icy roads or her father not taking proper care of his wound that would flare up at unexpected times. Work was what she needed; so she said, "If you'll engage the soldier over at the battalion who hires himself out as a waiter, I'll try having my first formal dinner. Colonel and Mrs. Tucker, Colonel and Mrs. Blaisdell, the Tillsons, and us. Do you think that would do, or should we have your captain and his wife, too?"

"It might be a good idea to include them—since we're having the Blaidsdells and Tillsons. Word gets around the outfit, you know."

"I kind of thought we should, so I'll plan for ten." Tippy set her glass on the table and jumped up to push his aside and sit on his lap. "I know now how Alcie felt, when we were down at her house last August and she gave her first party. I thought she acted sort of important and anxious, but I can understand, now, why she did. It's a very grave responsibility," she said, pressing his nose flat and leaning so close he looked at her cross-eyed. "I'll invite them for next Friday night."

She spent the following week shining silver and washing her best china and glassware. She laid out her new Venetian lace place mats and napkins, counting them over and over, to be sure the store had sold her mother an even dozen. She was at such a fever pitch by the morning of the party that Peter, starting off for a long day of tank warfare, kissed her good-by and said her blood pressure must be at a hundred and eighty.

"Listen, you boys," she said sternly to the dogs, wearing her oldest shorts and a halter, standing in the center of the living room with her vacuum cleaner. "Try. Please *try*—just for today—to keep your hair on."

Switzy hung out his tongue and Rollo rolled over on the divan. So she dropped her cleaning paraphernalia and went to find their comb. "See this?" she said, waving it at them. "I'm going to use it on you when I finish in here." And they got nimbly to their feet and padded out as a team.

It was four o'clock before the house suited her and vases were filled with fresh flowers; before the table was laid with twin candelabra holding new candles, before jellied consomme was seasoned and set in the refrigerator to chill, a pineapple prepared for the fruit salad, potatoes peeled and put in water, the roast beef ready in its pan. "Now." she said, and found her comb and a pair of scissors.

Two lean dogs emerged from under the house an hour later. Switzy was shorn down to his skin again. His topknot was a glory of brushed curls, the fluff left on his legs and hips made pantaloons, and a pompon adorned the end of his tail like a ball. Rollo hadn't fared so well. What hair he had lost had been pulled out through the teeth of the comb. Most of it was well attached to his skin, and he gave it up with protesting yelps. And he had no style. Whole pieces were missing from his tail where fur balls had been, and his scraggy sides caved in. He looked underfed and unloved, but he had two eyes. He could, so Tippy informed him, at least see where he was going.

"There," she said, hot and tired and covered with hair. "That's the best I can do. Kindly stay indoors."

The pink organza Peter liked was hanging on her closet door, waiting for just such an important occasion as this. A shower refreshed her and took the tiredness out of her bones. It turned her feathery curls into ringlets, too. It made her feel so good that she decided to take her time about dressing, dawdling a little while she turned Cinderella into a charming hostess. The messy part of her work was done, and one of the big aprons Trudy had given her would cover her up for the few things she had still to do. "Giving a party's a snap," she told her mirror. "All you have to do is be efficient."

It was almost six o'clock when she floated gracefully down the stairs, ready to give her immaculate living room an approving glance before she passed on to minor matters in the kitchen. Quite a sight met her eyes. Rollo lay on his back, paws up, on

the divan. Strands of what hair she had left in him strewed the
cushions and showed he had tried several spots before he found
the right place for his nap. Switzy had brought a greasy bone
home from somewhere, and was stripping it of fat in the middle
of the rug.

"I *did* close the kitchen door, I did, I know I did," Tippy
wailed, stamping her foot. "Get out of here, both of you! Look
what you've done!"

They lifted their heads, not to see the damage they had
wrought but simply to have a look at her and wag their tails.
Switzy's pompon quivered like a balance spring and Rollo's
skimpy plume sprayed the air with hair.

"Don't *do* that!" she cried with an agonized screech before
she grabbed them by their collars and dragged them out. She
threw the bone after them and slammed the door on their snarl-
ing over it, then ran to find her cleaning fluid and a whisk
broom. In her agitated energy she forgot it was time to put the
roast in the oven.

Peter found her on her hands and knees, scrubbing at a stubborn spot. "Everything looks beautiful," he praised amiably,
glad to be in out of the heat and dust, and stooping to press his
lips against the back of her neck which was the only kissable
spot presented to him. "What's the matter with the rug?"

She told him. Standing with her dust pan and cleaning rags,
she told him exactly what a nuisance dogs were, what a miserable, useless nuisance. "I've worked all day," she blazed wrath-
fully. "I've cleaned and cleaned and cooked and cooked, and
I'm so tired I want to sit down and cry. And now look at the
cushions—and *that!*"

The bottle of cleaning fluid bounced off the dust pan, and
Peter caught it in mid-air. "Nothing shows now, honey," he
said, taking the rest of her equipment from her. "I'll finish up

anything else you have to do. How about lying down awhile?"

"*Lying down?*" He had said the wrong thing. No hostess ever lies down an hour before her guests are due to arrive, with dinner still to cook, and Tippy told him so. "Why, the very idea," she cried wildly, pushing her hands through her curls and not caring. "How do you suppose all this got done? By lying down? And what do you think you're going to eat if I lie down?"

"Wup, wup, hold it." Peter sent her a grin. It was the best he could do with his hands full, so he said as soothingly as he could, "Take it easy, honey, I'll help you. If you'll tell me what you want me to cook. . . ."

"*The roast!* Oh, I forgot to put in the *roast!*" Tippy fled around the dining ell and across the kitchen. She snatched up the pan, shoved it into a cold oven, switched on the heat, and frantically tried to figure out what time dinner could be served, if ever, at this rate. At least thirty minutes of cooking time had been lost. What if she turned the heat up higher, would that help? she wondered. Or would it burn the meat to a cinder? What would a *good* cook do in such a crisis?

She was staring at the silent oven, willing fat to give a heartening sputter, when Peter pushed open the door. "Do you want me to go up and dress," he ventured, "or help you first?"

"Just dress."

He put the cleaning things in a cupboard under the sink and gave her a pat. "Chin up, childie," he said. "We'll make it. In a few hours people will be telling us it was a lovely party."

"I wish I could believe that," she said stiffly, still listening for some sound in the oven. "I'm sorry I was cross. I didn't mean to be."

"I know it, childie. I wish you weren't so tired."

"You'd better dress." A faint sputter, or perhaps just a hiss came to her, and she said, feeling better but still annoyed because he hadn't been here to help her, "Don't forget to clean the bathroom after you use it, and change your clothes in the den of horrors instead of the bedroom."

"O.K. I'll hurry."

She wasn't quite so nervous now. The roast was making beautiful noises and Peter was within call in case of an emergency. The soldier waiter would come soon, too; so all she had to do now was arrange the salad in a bowl, show him what plates to use, how to slice the icebox cake and add whipped cream, start the potatoes and asparagus, make the gravy—she supposed she could slip out to do that when the roast was done, if it ever was—and pop in the rolls. Crackers for the soup. . . . Where were the crackers?

She was on the kitchen stool, pawing among cans on a shelf when a familiar, choking odor reached her. "Peter!" she screamed, scrambling down and racing through the house. "The D.D.T. truck's coming! Close the louvers! Stop it! Tell the man he can't spray us tonight. *Do* something!"

Peter was in the shower, whistling under running water, so she slammed shut as many of the protective window coverings as she could before she ran back to close up the kitchen. Insecticide was already pouring in in a cloud. The rooms reeked of it, and the welcome odor of sizzling meat was lost in its choking stench.

"I'll take mosquitoes and window screens," she coughed, unrolling waxed paper and covering her long array of plates on the work counter. "Oh, why did I forget that this was the night for the darned old thing to come by? I could have closed up."

She fought her way back through the living room and could hear Peter sneezing away upstairs. She could see a car in the driveway, too, its windows closed, its occupants waiting for the fog to blow by.

"Peter?" she croaked. "The Tillsons are here." Then she remembered the glassless windows and ran upstairs to whisper, "The Tillsons are here half an hour too early. Are you ready?"

"Almost, but you aren't."

"I'll comb my hair again and just keep going out to the kitchen, I guess. Oh, why did I forget to close the louvers? You can't even breathe downstairs."

"It won't last long. I'll take a bath towel down and fan it."

The young Jordons seemed to be doing some sort of scarf dance in the living room when Lieutenant Colonel and Mrs. Tillson walked up the front steps and rang the bell. However, the host and hostess appeared in the hall together, panting a little but composed; and Mrs. Tillson looked into the lovely living room and thought, Imagine having time to dance before a party. Youth can accomplish wonders.

To Tippy, the evening began like a nightmare and followed the pattern straight through to the end. Nothing went as her mother's formal dinners had or even as she had confidently rehearsed hers; with interesting conversation ricocheting around the table and courses arriving on time. Long pauses occurred, and nothing arrived. Not until she went out and started something on its way. Even then, when the waiter finally did bring in a plate, he knocked knives and forks on the floor, trying to remove the one before it. The meal was served soldier style, more or less, Tippy thought drearily, giving Colonel Tucker her attention but too concerned with the piece of potato scooting off Mrs. Taylor's plate to hear what he said. And the food needed seasoning. Even the whipped cream tasted sour. Either sour or D.D.T.-ish. And it was so hot, so hopelessly, stiflingly hot.

She sat in her place with bright endurance, when she wasn't hopping up, disappearing, and coming back to smile again as if she hadn't been away, until the horrible, endless meal was over. The guests surreptitiously used the water in their finger bowls to wash beads of perspiration from their upper lips and took a last mop with their napkins before they pushed back their chairs. It was almost over. Just coffee in the living room, then they all could go home—and she could crawl into bed.

And then the lights went out. Just when everyone was standing about uncertainly, waiting for someone else to choose the best chairs and sit down first, the room was plunged into darkness. The tray of chattering coffee cups came to a stop. Voices murmured politely through the dark, "Sorry, I didn't know you were there"; and Tippy, the only one seated and reaching for a silver coffeepot on the low table before her, was left with her hands extended.

Peter groped his way to a window and opened the louver slats to see if lights in other houses were on. "They are," he reported through the gloom, "so I guess we just blew a fuse."

Just blew a fuse. Tippy stiffened. No one could see her in the dark so she sent him a glare. Why didn't he go rushing off to fix the fuse? She had been rushing off and fixing things all evening.

A little light came in and there was a great fuss of opening other windows. Whiffs of cool air blew in with the light to inform her in a breezy way of another dire omission. She had forgotten to open the louvers after the spraying was over. No wonder it had been so hot. She could almost feel the perspiration drying on her skin. "Darling," she said, rising to the emergency in her best hostess style, "will you ask Crawford to bring in the candles from the dining-room table?"

Crawford was right beside her but she couldn't see him. He

reminded her of his presence by nudging her with the tray. So Peter found his way to the dining room and came back looking like the Statue of Liberty, with lamps in two hands, and she felt an urgent desire to giggle. She wasn't mad at him any more, because he looked so sweet with his candles. She wished they could be alone in the dusk, their few evening dishes done and the record player going. But there sat all these uncomfortable people. The women mopping and the men looking as if they were about to have apoplexy in their uniforms. Oh, dear, she thought with a weary sigh, what *else* can happen? And at that moment Switzy and Rollo entered.

They didn't wait to greet the guests. Rollo headed for his favorite place on the divan, the one she occupied, and as he made his leap she could *feel* hair floating into the coffee cups. "Get down!" she whispered sternly, and pushed him off on the floor. Switzy turned into a clown and sat up to beg for sugar.

It was a pretty picture in the candlelight, Tippy and the two little dogs, but she didn't know it. Her guests did, and Peter. He proudly delivered the cups she filled and presented them with his pleasant grin and an air of deference that made the women quick to look up at him and smile. The men took their cups, said, "Thanks, Pete," and went on watching Tippy.

They didn't go home. Cool and comfortable at last, they sat and talked. Sleepily, Tippy wondered why. It was late and they should go home, she reasoned. After an evening such as they had suffered they should want to hustle home. She stifled yawns and watched the candles drip wax on her tables. She wondered if Crawford had done all the dishes or had left her some to wash, and wished she had the energy to slip out and see. No one would miss her, since they were doing what they should have done three hours ago, talking a mile to the minute, but she was too tired to get up.

Then there was a great commotion and sudden exclamations of, "Oh, dear, I didn't dream it was so late," and they were rising. "Such a delightful evening, dear," Mrs. Tucker said; and Mrs. Blaisdell, with an affectionate arm around Tippy's waist, told her, "We know we've stayed much too long, but that was because it was such a lovely party." Only the young captain's wife said slangily, "Gosh, you made the bust I invited you to look like a *wienie* roast." The men shook her hand and thumped Peter's shoulder.

The door was closed at last. Tippy stood beside a candelabrum coated with wax, and Peter came back to pick up the other one. "You didn't like me much tonight, did you?" she said breaking off a piece from a guttering candle. "You loved me but you didn't like me."

"Why, Tip, darling, of course I did." He set his candles down and came across to her but she quickly picked hers up.

"I didn't like you much when you didn't go and fix the fuse," she said honestly. "Just for a second."

"Well, I was proud of you."

"You couldn't have been. I was cross to you before the guests came, and I didn't apologize very pleasantly."

"It suited me."

"And the dinner was a mess. It was hot and smelly, and nothing went right."

"Listen, childie." Peter took her candelabrum and set it back on the table. "Everything was lovely," he said with his arms around her. "It was a beautiful dinner, and if anyone loused things up, I did. I didn't give you a bit of help and I should have known where the fuse box is and done something about the lights. I did sneak out to call the emergency electrician though," he said. "He'll have the current on before breakfast. Believe me, darling, it was a good party."

"You're sure?"

"Scout's honor."

"With forks falling on the floor and Mrs. Blaisdell's dessert clear over on the side of her plate? And Mrs. Tucker trying to get one of Rollo's hairs out of her mouth without anyone seeing her? And everyone hot? Oh, Peter, I'll be ashamed to write to Mums about it."

Her voice sounded so tired and ready to break that he picked her up in his arms and said, "You're going straight to bed, little girl. No cleaning up and fiddling around tonight. You've worked like a dog all day.'"

"Not like a dog," Tippy yawned, looking over his shoulder at Rollo, curled up on the divan, at Switzy, sniffing bonbons in a dish. "Those dumb dogs are what got everything going wrong."

"The boys," he reminded, blowing out the candles. "Boys will be boys. Come on, fellows, the Jordons are closing up shop."

There were no lights to turn out, so he carried her up the stairs, with two sets of paws padding contentedly behind.

CHAPTER XI

TIPPY was on the telephone early the next morning. The house was still in disorder, but she had to tell Molly about the party. So she kissed Peter good-by, closed the door on the dogs, and sat down on the cool tile in the hall.

"Everything was all fouled up," she said, when Molly asked the leading question, "How did it go?" "I feel as if I never can face those people again." And she gave lengthy descriptions of each episode as it had happened.

"Oh, gosh," Molly sent back, or "How awful," or "I thought he was supposed to be a good waiter." Appropriate comments that let Tippy say at the end:

"Just take a tip from Tippy. When you give your first party don't start out with the rank. Practice on the young bunch first. Get the hang of it before you try to be fancy. You know that girl I talk about so much, Alcie? My best friend and Peter's sister? Well, she gave a party last summer and it looked easy to me. I thought I could go her one better with my hands tied behind me, but I forgot that her mother-in-law sent her cook over and we ate outdoors and she had Jonathan to help her. And she hadn't any dogs and the fog truck didn't come by."

Molly had to laugh, even though her next words were sympathetic. "Poor dear," she said. "How would you like to go in town and forget it?"

"I'll go anywhere," Tippy answered, "where I won't run into Mesdames Tucker, Blaisdell, Tillson, and Taylor. I'll have to clean up this place, though."

"Could you be through by two?"

"I guess so." Tippy peeked around the living-room arch. The room was cluttered but clean, and the kitchen wasn't too bad. Peter had made the beds and helped her put away the good china, so she said, "I'll meet you at our favorite parking lot at two, and we'll leave one of the cars there. Let's get at our work."

Molly was always fun to be with. She had confessed to being a little homesick, too, but she lived so far away. To see her meant planning, not running in and out of each other's houses, drinking iced coffee in the mornings together and talking over an immediate problem. Tippy's neighbors were older girls with children and, while she sometimes saw them, they had their own sets of friends.

She and Molly shopped together. They explored the old part of Panama City, drove up and down its long, narrow streets crowded with open-front stores. Sometimes they sat in a park above the harbor, shielded from the hot sun by a semicircular monument that had been erected to honor all the engineers who had taken part in the building of the Canal, while her two dogs and the little dachshund, Heidie, chased each other over the gravel. Sometimes they drove through a fine residential section that was built on a bluff. Spanish-type houses overlooked the blue ocean in a nest of palm trees and flowers; and they drove up and down the hills, playing a game of choosing the ones they liked best, from the American ambassador's gleaming white mansion at the top to a perky little hacienda on the side of the cliff, looking as if it might let go at any moment and slide off into the sea.

Tippy learned the names of flowers and trees. She was grateful to the beautiful mimosa that offered its cool, fluttering shade, but she liked the royal palm tree best, because it was so neat and regal, and so different from the trees at home. Its encircling rings of growth were so precise, and it reared above the other palms in a truly royal way. The banana trees were chubby, fringe-leafed things that bore one bunch of fruit before they were chopped down and doomed to die, and the traveler palm was her very good friend.

"It always points its leaves North and South," Peter had told her, showing her the wide palm leaves spreading out flat, like a fan. "It's as good as a compass."

She had three on her lawn; and several times when she and Molly had been lost on strange roads, they had looked at other peoples' traveler palms and found their way home.

Tippy learned other things about Panama, too, and life in the Tropics. Some of them she learned the hard way, like forgetting to put her blue pumps in the dry closet where an electric coil always burned, and finding them covered with mold; and starting off for a walk across the baseball field to a bridge luncheon at the Officers Club, and having the sky do one of its sudden tricks with rain. Dry season or rainy, the Panamanian sky was apt to burst into tears, and Tippy learned how important an umbrella could be, or the cellophane raincoat she packed in a purse.

It was a humid climate, hot and enervating; the kind Trudy always said made people "do-less." Tippy learned not to labor in the heat of the day and not to expect others to rush at things with zeal. Clerks in the stores took their time. There was no hurry. A golden sun would rise again tomorrow. Small, old-fashioned buses made frequent stops and blocked the fast, American cars for minutes at a time while passengers alighted on hot, reluctant feet and lazily lifted out their market baskets.

Tippy wore full cotton skirts and white peasant blouses for coolness, a sheer rayon or a linen dress when she went to town, and her legs and arms and face became just a shade or two lighter than a new copper coin.

She liked her home. She liked Saturday afternoons and Sunday when Peter was there, but there were many times when not even Molly's chatter or a party could take away the homesickness and boredom that seemed to be a permanent, daytime lump in her throat.

"I love being married to Peter," she told the dogs one afternoon, stretched out in an old wicker chair because they occupied the swing. "I think I like the army. I always have—but I don't like being so far away from home." They were the only ones she had to talk to, even though they didn't care how she felt; so she told them, "I don't want Peter to find out how lonesome I am. It would only make him unhappy and it wouldn't do any good. You don't think he sees it, do you?"

Rollo took a sudden nip into his ragged fur where something itched and Switzy lifted his head to help if needed, then they both lay down again.

"I guess he doesn't," Tippy said with a sigh. "I hope not."

Peter knew far more about her than she thought he did. For one thing, he knew that the pictures of her family had never been unpacked. They still lay in one of the lockers in the storage room; and whenever he mentioned them, she said in an offhand way, "Oh, I'll take them out later. I don't know just where I want to put them, yet."

Kenneth Prescott's picture was somewhere in the pile; and sometimes Peter wondered if the other pictures stayed hidden because of it, because it was Ken's picture that she couldn't find a place for. Once he tried to ask her. He got as far as saying, "It seems queer not to have your family around. You had family faces all over the place at home."

"I know," she answered, "but I'm not at home." And she pushed the little trunk into a corner.

She couldn't say, "I'm so homesick now that I don't dare have Mums and Dad and all the others where I can see them. I'd burst into tears." So she only shrugged. She had forgotten Ken's picture was there.

Peter couldn't know that. He only knew she was restless, since the house was finished, hunting up things to do, gay and high-strung, nervous and too thin.

He was so contented. Tippy, his job, his home, were all he wanted or needed. He liked his new assignment; and he went off into the heat each morning, one of thirty-four young lieutenants in a tank battalion, pround of B Company and his own platoon. He was learning more and more about tank combat every day, and he came home at night, grimy, dusty, whistling, and wishing he could make Tippy as happy as he was. He wondered where and how he failed.

He was sure the fault lay within him, in things he either did or failed to do, for Tippy had never been the butterfly type of girl who demanded attention or needed to be constantly on the go. She was quiet and happy, childishly interested in simple pleasures and people. Now she stayed alone too much. It worried him. He brooded about it when he was away from her and had time to think; and whenever he could, he left the troop a little early, just to see her come running toward him, her arms outstretched and giving little skips of joy.

He didn't know she ever cried until one afternoon when he had driven home early with a friend. "Thanks for the lift," he said on the front walk. "It's my turn to pick you up tomorrow."

And because the dogs padded out to meet him from under the house, he knew Tippy was in her accustomed place in the swing, and went across the spongy grass.

She was sound asleep. Her curls were hot and damp on her forehead and the fist tucked under her cheek held a wad of cleansing tissue. Peter bent to kiss her and saw the marks of tears.

He thought they were tear streaks, and he was sure they were when his lips brushed hers and brought her upright in complete confusion. "Oh," she said, "I didn't expect you. Oh, my!" And she scrubbed at her cheeks and eyes much too hard as she tried to draw his attention away from her face to her skirt. "Just look at me," she scolded herself disgustedly. "All rumpled. I'm so hot I'm melting, and I meant to be cool and fresh when you came."

She gave an elaborate yawn that didn't fool him and swung her feet to the floor. He knew she wanted to run, so he blocked her way and said, "I got off a half-hour early today. I thought we might go for a drive and have dinner in town." The words popped out and weren't at all what he wanted to say. They were a compromise. They slid around the issue and offered a treat instead of a heart-to-heart talk that might straighten things out.

He wanted to be close to Tippy, to see into her mind and share her heart. If she had to cry, if there had to be unhappy times when the tears must come, he wanted it to be with his arms around her, sharing whatever grief she felt and easing it with his love. "Tippy, darling," he pleaded, "is there anything I can do?"

"You can get the ice out for whopping big glasses of ginger ale," she laughed, lifting her arms for him to pull her up. "And you can put on shorts and eat in our own dear house, as we'd both rather do. This is the darnedest, *hottest* climate."

She stood beside him, smiling, bubbling again like a happy little tea kettle, beads of moisture on her short upper lip. She had hoped he wouldn't notice the telltale traces of tears, but his face showed he had, so she went on brightly, "Molly and Al are driving over this evening, not to dinner, just to see us. Molly bought a Guatemalan skirt she wants to show me."

The moment was lost, as dozens of others had been, and each knew Tippy was the one who had pushed it away. She felt she had done it nobly, to spare him the histrionics of a silly bride who was too spineless to accept the life she had chosen; and as they went into their house together, she silently vowed, "I'll do better from now on. I'll never let him catch me crying again —and I'll like Panama if it kills me."

Peter's thoughts were more sober. It was up to him to wait and watch, he decided. Perhaps, someday, if he kept on trying, she would open her heart to him. She would be all his. Then the pictures could come out of the trunk, even Ken's.

The days went on into March, and he didn't see any sign of tears again.

Tippy was careful to cry in the mornings, or not cry at all if she could help it. Whenever the overpowering homesickness settled in her chest she took the dogs for a walk. Trudging along, she would tell herself sternly, "You'll have to be your own doctor. You know what's the matter with you, you're just being a baby. Stick to your medicine. Use some psychology on yourself, you dope. You're happy, aren't you? You want to stay with Peter, don't you? Of course you do. Why, what would you do without him? You were wretched in New York until he came back. You thought you couldn't stand it until he married you and brought you down here. Honestly, you're about the silliest girl I've ever met."

Her head always came up after a rightful self-scolding and she would stop kicking pebbles to look around her at the beauty, to really see it through the tiring heat. "Oh, golly," she would groan, "if only I'd have a letter from home today," and start all over again.

The house took so little of her time. The daytime parties she went to took less and were all the same. Girls talked of formulas and babies, the price of food and which post exchange held what. The older women played bridge. Tippy sat and listened courteously to whatever group she found herself in, continually hoping for an interesting conversation that she could relate to Peter when five o'clock came. She seldom heard any that she thought worth repeating, and her companions considered her a pretty little thing, but dull. Over their morning, after-marketing coffee in each other's houses, they sometimes discussed her and wondered what she sat and thought about.

Tippy could have told them. She thought about Peter and how much longer it would be until her watch said five o'clock and she could go home. She compared the girls with Penny, too, and with Alcie. Sitting with her big eyes on them she would think, Penny has children but she doesn't cram them down your throat all the time. And Alcie cooks. She just cooks. She doesn't sit around passing out recipes like handbills. They both talk about books and interesting events and things they're doing, and intelligent people. Maybe these girls think their children are intelligent people, though.

No, the parties didn't help. She came home from them full of sandwiches and sweet desserts but with her mind unfed, and with nothing more to talk about than when Peter had left her that morning. He had tales of tanks, a soldier who broke his leg, and a reconnaissance trip up the Changris River where he saw live alligators, and orchids growing in the trees. "And what did you do, childie?" he would ask; and she could only sigh and shake her head.

"Nothing much," she would answer. "I went to another party." And that was the end of her story.

She wrote to Penny about the parties, and the boredom, and the long hot days. She poured it all out on her new stationery splashed with tears, then settled down to wait for Penny's comforting reply. It didn't occur to her that Peter was the one to whom she should complain. She forgot that he had said, "We'll work things out together." She simply rushed out to mail the letter to Penny and wait impatiently for consolation.

She wondered why Penny took so long to answer; and as the days went by with nothing important in the mailbox beside the front door, she grieved a little harder because she had been so quickly pushed aside and forgotten.

Penny had gone to her mother with the letter. It was a windy, rainy day, unlike the sunny one Tippy was spending under her beautiful royal palm; and she said reluctantly, waiting for her mother to look up from the blotched pages, "Something is very wrong with our child. What do you think it is?"

"I don't know." Mrs. Parrish sighed as she laid the sheets of paper on the coffee table and got up to prod the fire. "Let me think," she said, looking down at the flames she had started and trying to remember her own young days as an army bride. And she turned around to ask, "Are you sure she's really in love with Peter?"

"As sure as I'm standing here. It isn't Ken, if that's what you mean," Penny answered, rereading a few lines on the top sheet. "She adores Peter. She says here she's afraid he'll discover that she isn't as happy as she ought to be—and so am I. What if he's already noticed it and thinks she's still grieving for Ken? It's a pretty tough spot for the guy."

"I remember," Mrs. Parrish said thoughtfully, following her own train of thought, "how homesick I was, when I first went to a strange post with your father, down at the very bottom of Texas. I thought I'd die; and your father finally invited Mama to come down for a visit. She stayed almost a month and we went up to Illinois on leave the following summer. I was all right after that. Tippy's never been away from us before."

"But, good grief, she has *Peter!*" Penny never had felt a moment's loneliness from the day she had married Josh, so she shook a disapproving head. "I can't see why she'd be home-sick," she said.

"Because we're a close-knit family. We all depend on each other, you know that. I'm sure the child's suffering and not getting as much out of everything as she should, but I do wish . . ." Mrs. Parrish set the poker in its rack and came back to Penny ". . . I do wish I could be sure that Peter knows why," she said.

"I might write and tell him."

"No, you'd have to be very careful. They have to work out their own life." Mrs. Parrish sighed and picked up the lettter again.

"Could you and Dad go down?"

"We wouldn't. I've always thought it was wrong of Mama to come running." A gust of wind rattled the windows and she said, "Listen to it howl around the corner of the house. Foolish little Tippy, and dear little Tippy, too, because she loves us so much. She'll have to brave it out, Penny."

"What shall I say when I answer the letter?"

"What we'll all say. That things are fine at home, that we want her to be happy and make Peter happy, that marriage is for 'better or for worse,' and to be grateful that it's in 'health', not 'sickness'. Point out her blessings to her."

"It's going to be a hard letter to write. Tippy's always been the kind who takes things awfully seriously but never says much," Penny said with a worried frown. "I don't want to sound scolding or unsympathetic; and I do want to give Peter some sort of hint."

"Then take your time and don't rush into it. Weigh what you write. I shall." Mrs. Parrish folded the letter and said sensibly, "I'd like to show it to Dad. Stop worrying, darling. Girls get homesick in boarding school, at summer camp, or with jobs away from home. It's not a fatal disease, you know. It hurts like fury but it does pass in time. Let's have tea and dismiss it for this afternoon."

So that was why Tippy waited and waited for a letter that, when it finally did come, was the cheeriest lack of understanding she had ever read. She couldn't believe it. She had to read it twice before it made any sense to her at all, and then not much. Of course she loved Peter. Penny sounded like an idiot, telling her to show her love and be demonstrative. Of course she got a kick out of Molly, out of the dogs, the beastly heat, her house, smells along the water front. No one need enumerate her blessings like a laundry list and tell her to "file them away for future memories." She was filing them away as fast as she could. And in a sudden burst of anger at Penny for casting her aside like a worn-out sister who was no good as a baby sitter any more, she "filed away" the letter, too.

Whatever Penny had set out to do, she had done with a bang. Tippy threw herself against Peter that evening and wept with abandon, "Oh, darling, you're the only one who loves me! You're all I have in the world."

CHAPTER XII

For the whole next week, Peter tried to figure out what had made the change in Tippy. For there was a change. After those few, heartbroken words at the door, when she had told him he was all she had, she became crisp and self-sufficient. The shining wonder was gone from her eyes and she became completely sure of herself.

She brought books home from the post library: deep books on the discovery and history of Panama. *The Chrangris* was one of them, and it was the story of the river he had told her of fording, the river that began so far back in the jungle, man had never penetrated to its source. She seemed fascinated by the river, by the little group of islands so close in the harbor, by the life of Balboa who was the first white man to cross the Isthmus, by the political independence of the little republic; and she discussed them with such authentic knowledge every evening that he thought she could deliver a very instructive lecture at the Womans Club. She puzzled him and she worried him, too, for he missed his doting little companion. This new Tippy, spreading information with the intensity of an amateur artist slapping paint on a canvas wasn't half as much fun. He wondered why he had a new wife but lacked the courage to ask.

A worrisome little thought kept bothering him. It gnawed away in his mind like a troublesome mouse until, buttoning the cuffs on his khaki shirt one morning, he left a button halfway through its hole and went into the storage room. The little tin trunk was still in its corner. He stood looking down at it, biting his lower lip before he leaned over and slowly lifted the lid.

The pictures were still inside, their newspaper wrappings undisturbed. All but one. A crumpled paper tossed carelessly back told him that one was missing. With fearful fingers he tore little holes in the others. Parrish faces looked at him—and Ken's. Ken's picture was there. It was his own that was missing.

He dropped the lid and stood looking out into the sun-splashed yard, already presaging another hot day. Why was his picture gone? he wondered. Where was it? Why had Tippy taken his away from the ones she loved, and where had she put it?

He rubbed his hand thoughtfully along his chin, wishing he could say to the understandable little Tippy of his West Point days, "Hey, chum, I'm not in the trunk. Where am I?" He could have said it then. He could have walked right downstairs and asked her. Now, living with her and loving her so much more than he ever had thought he could, he skirted the "keep out" signs she put on the special corners of her mind. "You're scared, fellow," he told himself, staring through the slats and massaging his freshly shaved chin. "You're still scared of a guy she used to love and afraid you'll find out something you don't want to know. You'll have to hunt around for yourself."

The photograph wasn't in their bedroom, as he was sure it wasn't, nor was it in any of the rooms downstairs. He looked carefully as he went through to the kitchen and down the outside steps.

Tippy was hanging a row of olive-drab socks on the clothes-line under the house. "Thanks for the very good breakfast, Mrs. Jordon," he said lightly. "I may not be home for lunch today, so is it all right if I take the car?"

"Um." She turned around with a clothespin in her mouth, then nipped it onto the line. "Now, why on earth, do you ask me that?" she laughed. "I'm not going anywhere. And even if I were, which I'm not, you don't have to ask. You have a job to do."

"Seems as if you've already done one." He pointed to the line of socks and shorts and slips, but she shrugged and shook her head.

"Child's play," she said, fluffing out a nylon ruffle. "I wanted to put the wash out while it was still cool. In another hour you can think of me relaxing in my office, improving my mind."

She pointed to the swing with its table of books beside it; and Peter, turning for a perfunctory glance, found himself staring. His picture was on the table. Not in the leather frame that had last incased it, but in a cardboard, homemade affair that wouldn't mildew. "How come I'm under here?" he asked before he thought.

"Because I like to have you with me when you're away." Tippy picked up her wicker laundry basket and skirted a chair to stand before him. "I don't like to be alone from you," she said. "I need you every hour of the day."

"I'm glad to hear it. Oh, boy, am I glad!" A car horn honked in the street, and he said, disappointed, "Darn it, Jeff's come by for me. You may have the car after all, Mrs. Jordon."

"I don't need it." Tippy set her basket on her head and stood with it balanced, her hands on her hips. "The laundry depart-ment bids you good-by."

The horn blew again, and he had a quite unsatisfactory kiss, trying to reach under the basket without knocking it off. "Don't get into mischief," he said; and she retorted:

"How could I? With only the boys for company—and Balboa, who's been dead for hundreds of years? I'll be in this very spot when you come back."

He had to go but he thought of her all day. A letter from Penny, carefully addressed to him at B Company, 45th Battalion, instead of Block Four Hundred, kept her in his mind. Something must be very wrong, he thought anxiously, slitting the envelope, if Penny had to write him a private letter.

"*Peter darling:*" It began.

"*I suppose I may as well come right out and say this letter concerns Tippy. She's homesick, Peter. Now don't let it worry you. If you have, (and knowing you I think you have) just remember that Mums says it isn't a fatal disease. She says she had it when she was a bride and away from home for the first time, and we both feel it isn't Tippy's homesickness that matters so much—it's the way she behaves and its effect on you. Please believe me, Peter, it's just homesickness and nothing else. She adores you but she's an odd little thing. She's Parrish in so many ways, but more tense, more serious and introspective than the rest of us. She probably has a conscience complex, too, over leaving Mums and Dad alone, I mean, and she'll aggravate whatever loneliness she feels by worrying about them. And she has some sort of queer idea that girls' conversations are small and narrow, and that her doings wouldn't interest you. Goodness knows why. I wrote to her the other day. . . .*"

There was a whole page more, but Peter let the letter drop on his desk. He felt a mixture of emotions: relief, of a sort, because Penny had insisted that Tippy's loneliness was for her parents, not for what she might have had with Ken; doubt and sorrow, too, because he and Tippy were receiving counsel apart, on something they should share.

Two letters. Two people receiving them, yet not saying so. He read the last pages while he lit a cigarette, then folded them carefully and put them in the pocket of his coveralls. Penny was trying to be helpful, but no one could straighten out the snarl, save Tippy. She was at home reading her books, and he had a tank waiting in the shed and a crew to teach. Well, perhaps time would take care of things. He would see what he could do tonight.

A half-formed plan of entertainment began to take shape as he worked, a week end at a little lake he had heard of, up in the mountains; but it slipped out of his mind when he opened the front door and Tippy came running through the living room, his cold drink ready.

"Love me?" she asked, watching him rub the icy glass back and forth across his hot forehead.

"I do. And," he said before he took a swallow, "I like you, too. I like you very much."

"I'm glad. Sometimes I don't like myself so much."

"Why not?"

"Because I do such stupid things. Today, for instance. I meant to accomplish so much today—and I didn't."

He was hot and tired and needed a shower, but there was a chance that Tippy might give him an opening to pry into her hidden feelings, so he tossed his cap on a chair and went into the living room with her. "What threw you off the track?" he asked.

"I went to a silly party." She settled him in his chair, lighted a cigarette for him, and set a plastic coaster on the table for his glass. "I'd forgotten I was invited," she explained, sitting cross-

legged on the ottoman beside his feet. "I just happened to look
on my calendar, and there it was."

"Where?"

"At Midge's. Midge Ralston's, you know."

"No good?"

"It was awful." Tippy rested her elbow on her knee and
cupped her chin in her palm. "Why is it, Peter," she asked,
"that women's parties are so dull?"

"Are they? I never went to one."

"Girls talk of the dullest things," she went on. "At every
party—the same things. Today we listened for fifteen minutes
while Grace Rutledge told how little Beany threw his bowl
of cereal on the floor. It sloshed the rug and bounced straight
up again to splatter the drapes. I know the exact places in the
drapery pattern where it hit, and I can decribe the tea towel
she grabbed to mop it up with. It's her *best* one," she said
impressively. "It has red and white stripes, and it's *embroidered*.
And I can show you the triumphant look Beany gave her when
he leaned over his high chair and said, '*Too* bad, Mummy.'
And exactly how Grace slapped him."

Peter threw back his head and laughed. He laughed so hard
that Tippy glared at him. "Do you think that's funny?" she
demanded.

"It is when you tell it. And from seeing young Beany in
action around the repair shops, I can see why his mother socked
him."

"But it's so uninteresting," Tippy protested, looking puzzled.
"Suppose you came home at night with nothing better to talk
about than stuffed olive sandwiches and the fit a colonel's wife
had because she had to rip out a whole sleeve of the sweater she
was knitting? Or Beany Rutledge? You have interesting things
to tell."

"Lots of things are interesting, Tip." Peter set his glass down and tried to explain, "If I wanted man-talk or shop-talk all the time, I'd live in barracks. Why marry a woman?"

"I guess I hadn't thought of that."

"And if you wanted to know the army from the inside instead of catching glimpses of it by listening to me yak about it, you might as well have joined the WACs. We each have something to give the other. Your life with the girls is as important to us both as mine at the battalion is, childie. We bring our special brand of talk home, mix it up and either laugh at it or grumble over it, and—well, we sort of grow along together."

"I see." Tippy pinched a fold in the skirt of her lavender dress and pressed it over her knee. "Then you don't think these girls down here are—useless?" she asked without looking up. "I mean, they seem so dull. They never talk about books they've read or current affairs. I even wonder sometimes if they know Eisenhower's been elected President. Maybe they think he's still over in Europe, or that maybe Europe's fallen off the face of the earth, I don't know."

Peter grinned at the top of her bent head. "Childie," he said, leaning over and taking her hand in his, "people down here don't know each other very well. They have to have a common meeting ground. Women have kids, men have the army."

"But Molly and I. . . ."

"Sure. Molly and you. Jeff and I, or Todd and I, just two together, we talk about a lot of things. But a whole bunch? It's shop-talk mostly, or where we're going with our wives, or something funny. Our dinner party made a whale of a hit."

"You didn't *tell* it!"

"Why not? I thought it was a riot. I'll bet if you'd told it at that party this afternoon, no one would have cared how Grace got Beany's pablum off the floor."

"It wasn't pablum," Tippy giggled, "it was oatmeal with raisins in it." And she finally lifted her eyes to say, "I never thought of making fun of ourselves about the party. I was too ashamed. But it was kind of funny, wasn't it?"

"Ask Jeff, or Todd Mercer. Todd almost died laughing at Ma Tucker spitting out Rollo's hair. We call her Ma as the Colonel does," he said confidentially, "when he isn't around."

They were getting somewhere. Tippy's heart was beginning to open like a tight little bud. "Maybe I will tell it," she was saying when the telephone rang. "It's better to make a good story ourselves than have someone else do it," she laughed, scrambling up and going into the hall.

Peter took the last swallow of liquid that was warm now, listened idly to her say "hello"; then set his glass down with a bang as she cried, "Well, for mercy's sakes! Where are you?"

"Who is it?" he called; and pulled himself out of the chair to follow her.

"Gwenn. She's here!" She slapped the palm of her hand over the receiver and whispered above it, "At El Panama. Been there two days." And as dulcet tones continued to float out she took her hand away and exclaimed, "I can't believe it. Are you coming out? To stay with us, I mean?"

Peter bent double in his anxiety to hear an answer; and when Tippy shook her head at him and grinned he reached for the telephone, but she pulled it away. "I can't believe it," she said into the mouthpiece. "Really? Oh, my goodness, wait till I find Peter. Just hold on."

Her hand acted like a bottle cap again, and she leaned as far away from it as she could to call, "Oh, Peter?" Then in a lower voice she said, "Gwenn's mad at Bill. She's taking a trip. Perhaps around the world, she doesn't know. Shall I ask her out to dinner?"

"Lord, yes, I guess so. We'll have to get to the bottom of things. Let me talk to her."

"He's coming." Tippy flung out the words as the receiver changed hands. She even scuffled her feet to imitate the sound of someone walking.

"Hello, Gwenn." Peter's voice was gruffer than he meant it to sound, so he cleared his throat and said, "You sure surprised us. How about coming out? You will? O.K., I'll drive in and pick you up. Be there in twenty minutes."

Tippy watched him frown as he laid the telephone back in place. The Parrishes, he was thinking, keep nicely out of things, but here comes a Jordon. Penny writes us encouraging letters about the first year being full of adjustments and not to take it too hard, so here comes Gwenn to dump her troubles on us. "Gosh darn it," he grumbled, running his hand through his hair, "what does she have to follow us for?"

"Perhaps she needs us to help her." Tippy pushed him toward the stairs and ordered, "Change your clothes and go get her. I'll take my big thick steak I've been saving out of the freezing compartment and start dinner. Be nice to her, darling," she urged, knowing he didn't want Gwenn. Of the eight Jordons he could have chosen Gwenn would have been the last.

Laughter lights danced in her eyes as she set her table for three, for she was imagining a similar scene, had she dropped in on Bobby and his bride. "He'd slay me alive," she told the new sterling silver knives and forks as she laid them in place. "My life wouldn't be worth a plugged nickel."

She was secretly a little excited to be seeing Gwenn—the way Alice had felt when she proudly showed her new house. Gwenn was the first person from home to see how lovely it was; and while she wasn't exactly the one Tippy would have welcomed, either, she was still a person from home. She had two eyes and a voice, and she could look and admire. Or would she? Tippy knew she wouldn't the minute she flung open the door.

Gwenn came in reeking of all the perfume the hotel lobby must have had to sell. She wore sheer black and a high pearl choker. The pearls are real, Tippy thought, taking the mink stole, luxurious precaution against nights that sometimes do cool off in Panama. Her skin was a beautiful bronze, evidence that she had come on a ship not a plane, and her hair was the golden gold of the movies.

"It's sweet of you to ask me out," she said, dropping into Peter's favorite chair and not looking around at all. "What a perfectly horrid climate! If I'd known how beastly hot it is, I shouldn't have bothered to come."

Tippy forgot she had ever disliked the climate, too, and rushed to its defense. "It's wonderful after you're used to it," she said, knowing her face was faintly perspiring from the heat of the stove, and wondering how Gwenn, although only two years older, always managed to make her feel so young and gauche. "Peter will bring us something cool to drink and I can open the louvers more now."

"Don't bother." Gwenn leaned back in her chair and let her hands hang limply over its arms. "Nothing matters," she said dramatically.

Tippy glanced sharply at Peter. She knew with wifely instinct what he was about to say; and since it was what all the Jordons had constantly said through the years, "Oh, Gwenn, be yourself," she shook her head at him. "Darling," she said, letting him see the prideful shine of love in her eyes, "take out some ice cubes for me."

He started for the kitchen but stopped in the turn of the

ell to shrug his shoulders and spread his hands in a flat gesture that was meant to convey to Tippy his complete confusion about the whole affair, even after half an hour in the car with the cause of it.

Tippy loved his expression. He was counting on her to do something about this situation, either to eliminate it or straighten it out, and she felt proud. Up to now she had leaned on him and his sturdy masculine decisions. He was the one who had promptly sent a truck to town for the furniture when the store didn't deliver it on time; he had found men to shine the tiled floors and wash the woodwork. He managed men.

As he had pointed out with such reasonable patience, there were two sides to every marriage. The masculine side and the feminine side. Well, Gwenn was a woman. She was hers to handle; and Tippy turned back to her with relish.

CHAPTER XIII

"So that's the way things stand," Gwenn said, fitting a cigarette into a holder long enough to be a fishing pole. "Bill Hanley may be a star, he may be in line for an Oscar on his latest picture, but he can't own me."

She had talked steadily for four hours. She had sat spinelessly in her chair, fitting cigarettes into the holder, or had prowled about the room with a pantherlike tread. She had talked so incessantly and without listening that Peter had given up and gone to bed.

Her whole scene was well rehearsed and must have been repeated many times. Now and then she reminded Tippy of an orator who, having lost his place in his speech, had to go back and pick up a paragraph or two. She went through it the same way Penny said she could do *A Month of Sundays* by now, without too much concentration and her mind on something else.

"What do you think?" she asked so suddenly that Tippy jumped.

"I think you're being foolish." Tippy had been asked, so she answered. "I don't doubt that Bill's all wrapped up in himself," she said, "and vain, and arrogant, and important. So are you."

"Really!"

She didn't say the word as Americans usually pronounce it, to rhyme with mealy, nor did she use the broad *a* she was so fond of. She said *rally*. The first time she had snapped it out Tippy thought she was supposed to assemble her wits and do something spectacular, so had sat up and taken a breath to speak. The preparation was as far as she went, for Gwenn's continued flow of complaint made it plain that the expression was merely an exclamation, not a command. So now she shrugged.

"You asked me," she said. "You and Bill lead a hectic kind of life. It isn't a normal one."

Tippy had been in and out of more Hollywood night clubs in one evening than she could personally visit in a year. She knew dozens of stars by their first names, had gone to sumptuous parties in their homes, dined on Sèvres china, had had a private showing of all the secret vices and petty jealousies which seemed to fill their lives, until she began to wonder what had become of the nice, normal people Penny had met when she made a picture there. The ones Gwenn had introduced her to were as flighty and unbalanced as she and Bill were. "Have you ever tried settling down and making a home for Bill?" she asked.

"Me?" Gwenn flared. "You know I'm a dancer. I studied with Marenka Savitskaya in New York, and I should be in musicals. Every time I'm almost offered a part Bill steps in and blocks it."

She waved her fascinating holder and made a perfect smoke ring with it. The holder was about the only thing that kept Tippy awake, for it was constantly falling off an ash tray or spraying hot ashes on the rug. As a fire hazard it matched the inflammable Gwenn, for she was just as destructive in her own way and left nothing but a trail of smoke behind her. Tippy hoped they would both burn out eventually and retire to the pretty guest room.

"You might as well spend the night," Peter had said with a yawn when he gave out. "I have a tactical problem tomorrow and Tippy'll drive you in." So one of Tippy's trousseau nightgowns was spread out on the lovely hand-painted bed, and her new purple Guatemalan skirt and blouse lay over a chair.

Gwenn had accepted the room with a condescending shrug and a laugh as rueful as her glance around, as she said, "It seems frightfully foolish to pay fifty dollars a day for a suite at El Panama, then sleep out here. I can see dear Bill pointing that out to me. But thanks anyway. I do have a lot more I want to talk about."

She was still performing. Hunger had sent Tippy to the kitchen for large wedges of cake, which she sat and ate while Gwenn watched her. Gwenn was mindful of her figure that was built along the lines of her cigarette holder but secretly envious of the curves Tippy had in all the right places and a waist Peter's two hands could span. "I don't see how you do it," she said, watching a large piece of chocolate icing disappear into Tippy's mouth. "Bill would have a fit if I touched a piece of cake."

"Well, he isn't here to see it. Have one."

Tippy held out the plate but Gwenn looked away from temptation. "I couldn't," she said, and reached for her gold cigarette lighter instead.

Tippy sighed. Gwenn was lighting up again so release was not in sight. "If I were you," she said, licking the last crumb from her fingers and offering one more suggestion, "I'd either accept Bill as he is and try to make a place for myself as a hostess or I'd go off on my own and land a part. If I wanted to be in the movies, I'd be in the movies. Nothing could stop me. You see, Gwenn," she explained earnestly, "we have to know what we want. You ran off and married Bill on impulse."

"I knew what I wanted."

"Then why not make the best of it?" She wished this were Alcie facing her. Alcie's big gray eyes would understand what she meant. Alcie had been so hurt and grieved when Gwenn had eloped with a boy she scarcely knew. "You married Bill," she repeated.

"Naturally. Or so I've been led to believe for four years." Gwenn snapped the lid of her lighter shut and said with unexpected vehemence, "How could you ever understand? You never had any ambition. You were always content to bask in Penny's glory and never tried to do anything for yourself—neither you nor Alcie. I used to wonder how you both could bear to be so lazy and what you thought you were making out of your lives."

Tippy was given a piece of stage and some lines of her own to say, so she spoke up quickly. "We always wonder that about ourselves and other people, Gwenn," she said. "I do, every day. I know I want a life with Peter. I wouldn't trade places with you, or Penny, or Alcie, or anyone else, so my problem is to make a good life out of the one I've chosen. I'm not sure I've been doing it, but I'm working at it. Sometimes," she said, remembering her talk with Peter before Gwenn had interrupted it, "we have to change our ideas. We—we learn by listening to the other half of the marriage."

"Not me." Gwenn snatched the conversation back where it belonged, conscious of having lost her audience. One wrong cue and Tippy's mind had transferred itself to something else. Gwenn couldn't bring it back, so she yawned and said, "I'm tired. Suppose we go to bed. Let Mr. Hanley play about in his

WELCOME HOME, MRS. JORDON

Miami hotel while I suffer. Who cares?" And Tippy almost pushed her up the stairs.

Dear me, it's after two o'clock, she thought, stumbling about in the dark, not to waken Peter. Six o'clock comes so early.

She felt the back of the clock to be sure the alarm was set, and had only just closed her eyes it seemed when its cheerful scream sat her up again in bed.

Breakfast to cook. For a moment she forgot Gwenn, rumpling her pink percale sheets in the guest room, while she stumbled across the floor, rubbing the sleep from her eyes. Only Peter's whisper through the bathroom door reminded her.

"My shined tanker's boots are in the guest room dry closet," he said. "What'll I do?"

"I'll get them."

She replaced her toothbrush in the medicine cabinet, ran a quick comb through her hair, and tucked her red-and-white striped blouse into her white skirt before she tiptoed into Gwenn's room.

Gwenn lay on her side. She looked younger with her make-up off. She looked almost as she had when she used to come clopping down the stairs on Governors Island, her curls tumbled, her face shining from soap and water and a good night's sleep. "What a pity it is," Tippy sighed, taking the shoes and sneaking out, "that she can't always look this way."

Peter had the coffee on when she reached the kitchen, and they talked in low tones while she fried bacon and eggs. "I wish to goodness she'd move on with her cruise," he said, sitting down and stamping his foot into a shoe. "Scoot, Switz. Tippy'll give you your breakfast. Did she say what her plans are?"

"She doesn't seem to know." Tippy set two bowls of bread

and milk side by side near the door and looked around to say over her shoulder, "Wasn't she a riot when she saw Rollo? I thought she was going to jerk right out of her pearl collar. And wasn't he horrid to growl at her? He acted as if he remembered how she used to dislike him."

"She was always giving him the pitch." Peter tried to lower his voice again, and said as he finished lacing his boot, "What do you say to eating outside? She's right up above us and I can't go on whispering forever."

So they carried trays down the steps, into their cool, airy room. Tippy sat in the swing and Peter hunched over the low table, in the padless wicker chair.

"What all did she say?" he asked. "I mean, was there anything different from the harangue I heard?"

"It was all pretty much the same, except. . . ." She took time to spread a piece of toast with jam before she expressed what she believed to be the point of Gwenn's visit. "She's in love with Bill," she said. "Of course she's jealous of him, terribly jealous of his success, I mean. I know it sounds awful to say it, but from things she let slip, I know it isn't Bill's fault that she can't get a part in a musical. She just isn't good enough, Peter. You have to be good. And you and I know she won't start at the bottom. She's married to a star—and she wants to march into a studio and be one, too. I'm sure Bill's cushioned the blow by pretending he doesn't want her to act. I don't like Bill but I do think he's tried."

"I have a feeling you're right. But what I want to know is— what's she planning to do?"

"Pour me some coffee." She held out her cup and said as he filled it from the aluminum percolator, "They had a fight. It must have been a dilly from the things she says they said to each other, and she flounced off. She'd show him. Now she doesn't know how to get back."

"Can't she fly?"

Tippy joggled her cup and spilled coffee into its saucer from laughing. "Dear idiot," she said, bending over the little table to kiss his sun-bleached hair, "it isn't a matter of transportaton. They had a fight, remember? He has to *beg* her to come."

"I wouldn't do it." Peter laid down his toast and declared, "I'd let her go around and around the world till she got dizzy before I'd ever ask her to come back."

"Would you do that to me?"

"Huh?"

"If we had a quarrel," she asked over her tray, "would you let me go away and stay forever?"

"Yep." He looked across at her and grinned. "In the first place," he pointed out, "we wouldn't have that kind of a quarrel. Or if we did, it would mean we had reached the end and there was no use trying any more. If you said you couldn't take it any longer and wanted to leave, I'd believe you. I'd know you had good reasons and I'd wonder what was wrong with me. I'd do everything in my power to make you happy," he said. "I wouldn't want to let you go."

"Oh, darling." Tippy plopped her cup into its saucer and clasped her hands under her chin. "I do love you so much," she said, studying his face. "I couldn't ever leave you."

"You will if we don't get rid of her." He pointed upward.

"That's what she wants us to do. I figured it out." Tippy set her tray on the floor beside the swing and tucked her bare legs under her as she explained carefully, "We're supposed to call up Bill and tell him where she is so *he'll* call *her*."

"That'd be darned expensive. I don't mind kicking a hole in the budget if I thought we could find him in one try, but how could we? One minute he's biting his nails over winning an Oscar in Hollywood, then he's taking bows in Twenty-one and The Stork in New York. He even runs down to give Miami a treat."

"That's where he is right now. Gwenn mentioned the name of his hotel about fifteen times after she really warmed up and was sure I understood her desperate situation. She practically drilled it into me so I wouldn't forget. It's the Cheltham."

"And we're supposed to spend our good dough and call him up?"

"Umhum."

"You do it. I'd have to wait till tonight and goodness knows where the will-o'-the-wisp might have flown by then. Let's treat ourselves to daytime prices and get it over. Let's see her off with rejoicing."

"He may not want her," Tippy said hesitantly. "What would I do about that?"

"It's your job to make him." Peter scooped the last bite of egg from his plate and stood up. "Sell her to him, childie," he begged. "I want to be alone with you again."

"I'll do my best."

She carried her trays inside after he had gone and wondered if a one-sided conversation would wake Gwenn. She could talk very low, but she might have to talk a lot. Finally she took the telephone inside the hall closet and closed the door.

It was stifling in there, with the electric coil glowing a busy, bright red, and she had to sit down and unscrew it. She had to open the door a little, too, after she had given the operator her call and during the interminable time that followed.

"I hope he isn't cross when people wake him up," she mumbled, pushing Peter's long raincoat out of her face. "I need him good-natured."

It took eighteen minutes to complete the call and she was almost asleep when Bill Hanley's voice roused her. He wasn't happy about being wakened. She could tell that from the cross way he spoke to the girl at the switchboard, so she plunged right in. She did it the way she used to hold her nose and dive into icy water, without waiting to think.

She talked fast. She painted such a tragic picture of Gwenn, distraught and lonely, that the black sheer began to look like mourning garb and even she was filled with pity. But Bill stayed unconvinced. He was too noncommittal. His silences and her flow of words were costing money. Then she thought she heard someone moving about upstairs and had to waste more time to open the door and listen. Gwenn was just starting down the steps.

"All right!" she cried, slamming shut the door again and boiling from both frustration and the heat. "If that's the way you want to act, good-by. Someday you'll be sorry, though." And down went the receiver with a bang.

She mopped her dripping face on her sleeve and went crawling out with her telephone. "Good morning," she said, flapping her shirt so the cool air could dry it. And to explain her strange appearance from a closet, she added, "I had a call to make and I didn't want to disturb you. How about some breakfast?"

"I never eat it." Gwenn paused with her hand draped over the newel post and asked remotely, lost in thoughts of her own, "Can I call a cab from here? I want to go back to the hotel."

She looked really pretty. There hadn't been enough cosmetics in her little evening bag to do much damage to her face; and Tippy said impulsively, "You should use just lipstick, Gwenn, your skin's so lovely. I'll drive you in if you really have to go."

"I do. I'm tired of Panama and I want to ask about planes for somewhere else. I may try South America."

The housework would have to wait. Tippy packed Gwenn's dress in a box and got out the car. They drove through the blazing sunlight together, Gwenn almost silent, Tippy conscience-stricken and afraid she might have misunderstood her veiled instructions and done more harm than good. The lateness of the hour and her sleepiness might have put her off the track, she worried. What if Gwenn didn't want to go back? Oh, dear.

She tried to find a way to confess her interference, and it wasn't until they swept up a driveway and stopped behind the white hotel that she found the courage to say, "Gwenn, listen a minute. If Bill should call you up and want you to come back —be nice to him. I know he loves you. I could tell it at my wedding."

Gwenn's only answer was a cryptic smile. It looked to Tippy like the smile of a very pleasant cat that liked little canaries for breakfast. And she gave her box to a bellboy, before she turned to ask, wide-eyed and innocent, "How would he know where to find me?"

"Well, he—I. . . ."

"Thanks for being so nice to me last night. I'm glad you and Peter are happy."

"Will you let us know what you plan to do?"

"When I decide." The bellboy still held the door open and she stepped out into a patio, green with plants and palm trees. "Thanks again," she said, swinging away with her pantherish, head-high walk that made her always distinctive in a crowd.

The walk, the make-up, the extravagant speech. Tippy knew those were the things in Gwenn that held Bill to her; and she thought about them as she drove slowly homeward. They were such shallow, surface things. They wouldn't appeal to Peter. He would look below them, straight into the empty shell.

She pulled her car off to the side of the road and sat looking toward the rolling mountains. There went the Changris, flowing into the sea from its secret source; there went a freighter, passing through its last lock and on its way to blue adventure. Somewhere over there was Peter. Beyond the Miraflores Bridge, on that low spot of flat terrain, he was baking in the heat while he proved the mobility of a war tank.

Her thoughts reached out to him. He knew something she wanted very much to learn.

"I think I'll drop by Midge's and have second coffee," she suddenly decided, starting her car. "I can clean up the house any old time."

It was a new and novel idea to her, and it led to an unexpected trip across the Isthmus to buy a portable washing machine Midge needed. It involved two other girls and lunch in the Navy Club, plus a thorough inspection of all the stock in the unusual commissary, so that Tippy was just putting her kitchen in order when she heard Peter say good-by to Jeff.

"Where is she?" he called, not waiting to hit the top step.

"I don't know." Tippy and her glass of cold ginger ale were coming too fast for safety. "I left her at the hotel," she said, slowing down. "She said she might call us when she knows her plans."

"Did you reach Bill?"

"Oh, I talked to him—at least eight dollars worth, from what the operator told me the first three minutes would cost. At first he was mad and wouldn't listen. Then he calmed down a little, and just when I thought I might begin to get somewhere, Gwenn comes tripping down the stairs. I had to hang up."

"Shall we call her?"

"After you cool off. You look like a ripe tomato."

Tippy held the glass out to him but he sat down on the bottom stair step. "She might come back," he said. "Mrs. Jordon, will you do me the honor of dining at the club with me?"

"Perhaps," Tippy sat down beside him and leaned her chin on his shoulder. "You're always so kind to everyone," she said. "It isn't like you not to want Gwenn to inconvenience us."

"I know it, honey." He reached for the glass and took a long swallow. "I'd welcome Alcie or Jenifer, because I know they're good for us," he said slowly. "They'd bring us happiness. Gwenn—I don't like a gal who can't take it on the chin, who's selfish and sly. Gwenn didn't come to see you or me or our house. She came for the reason you spotted. Well, we've done what she wanted and I'll bet she knows it by now. If she does go back to Bill, we won't hear from her again for ages. That's Gwenn. And I don't want her imposing on you."

"She can't do that, darling. You must remember that I've known her for years and years, too. To quote Trudy again, 'She did me good and helped me, too.'" Tippy got up and went to the telephone. "I'll just check on her," she said, giving El Panama's number; and she told Peter about her stay in the closet while she waited. "Oh, golly, I forgot to turn the coil back on," she said. "Screw it in for me." And in a louder voice she asked, "Will you ring Mrs. Hanley, please? Mrs. William Hanley. Oh, she has? Did she leave a forwarding address? Miami? Thank you very much."

"Well!" Peter said on his hands and knees in the closet. "As I mentioned before— that's Gwenn for you. She's gone."

"And my purple skirt and blouse went with her." Tippy had to laugh. "We lost eighteen dollars today, Lieutenant," she said, "so Mrs. Jordon cannot accept your kind invitation to step out and dine. Beef stew at home we are having."

They laughed quite a lot over their simple supper. Everything belonged to them again. Peter tied up vines in the evening twilight and Rollo and Switzy trotted off to meet their favorite guard. Tippy sat on the grass, elbows resting on the bottom step, and was surprised to discover how short and pleasant the day had been.

CHAPTER XIV

TIPPY sat on the floor in Grace Rutledge's cluttered living room. Coffee cups littered the tables and a long length of pink embroidered material stretched across the floor. Molly was on her hands and knees, figuring out how to cut it into a skirt without ruining the pattern, and Midge stood tapping a baby's bottle of milk against the palm of her hand.

"Well, bless me," she said, looking down at Tippy and forgetting she had been on her way to give the bottle to a Panamanian girl, sitting on the front steps, staring at a baby carriage in a half doze. "Why haven't you ever told us Penny Parrish is your sister?"

"I never thought of it," Tippy answered. "If you hadn't mentioned seeing her play, I wouldn't have thought of it now."

"Imagine actually knowing her," Grace said, laying down Beany's little shirt she was mending. "What's she like?"

"Us," Tippy returned promptly. "Just exactly like us." And she leaned back against the shabby couch to say with truthfulness, "I've never thought of it before but Penny fiddles with little Parri and Joshu, and her housekeeping and parties, just the way you all do. Why, she *is* like us. She's smart enough to know it, too."

She remembered Penny's letter, hidden away in a drawer at home, and was glad when Midge said, "Don't tell anything more until I take this to Rosaline." It gave her a chance to think about Penny. Wonderful, understanding Penny. A wave of sadness swept over her; but little Beany tripped over her feet and turned it to laughter. "Brrr," she growled, and rolled him over to tickle his stomach.

She was one of the girls. They liked her. They thought she was interesting. But best of all, she liked them, too. Grace Rutledge had surprised her earlier in the afternoon by saying, "My mother would have a fit if she could see how lazy I am. She faithfully mails me all her Book-of-the-Month-Club selections, and I just let them stack up. Perhaps it's the heat or having a maid for the first time in my life, but I'm certainly taking life easy. I don't even keep on my diet."

She was much too fat, squashed down in her chair, Tippy thought, but she was always smiling. And she whisked after Beany on long thin legs that looked like pipestems.

Midge was thin and nervous, black of hair and sharp in her movements. She was the one who had said with a sigh, "I never have time enough to read. Not even with a daytime nurse for the baby. It's hurry, hurry, hurry!"

"So you can load up your groceries and run over here for another cup of coffee," Grace had put in comfortably.

"So I can keep ahead of myself," she retorted. "Honestly, I think I accomplished more when Mark was stationed at Camp Kilmer. We went to New York a lot oftener than we go in to Panama City. We did all the museums and saw all the new plays. Gosh, I'd like to see one, *now!*" And that was when she had mentioned Penny Parrish.

Once Tippy started talking it was easy to bring Penny to life. "I have some pictures of her," she said, after Midge came back and Grace asked if she and Penny looked alike. "I'll show them to you when we have a session at my house. How about Monday? Peter's always home on Saturday afternoon, so how about coming over on Monday?"

"That's the day of Peggy Greer's luncheon," Molly looked up from her cutting to remind. "Tip and I met her on the ship, and she's so filthy rich and such a fool about it that we'll probably eat off of gold plates and have perfumed water in the finger bowls, but we have to go. Shall I take a chance and cut this piece off?"

"Whack it. No, not there, an inch farther on." Tippy leaned over and placed the scissors in position. "Tuesday, then." Her watch on her outstretched wrist caught her eye and she scrambled up with her plate and cup. "Why, it's almost five o'clock!" she exclaimed with surprise. "I'd no idea it was so late. Peter'll be coming. Oh, dear, I have to hurry."

She snatched up other plates and ran to the kitchen with them over Grace's placid protests. Molly rolled up the rest of her uncut material and picked up stray ravelings while Midge removed the worst clutter of all, a baby's traveling equipment. No trained army could have broken camp more quickly or with such chatter.

"Tuesday," Tippy called, the first to pull her car away from the curb.

"Oh, what if Peter's already home," she worried, turning away from Termite Row and swinging around the corner. "He won't know what to think if I'm not there."

Rollo and Switzy blocked the driveway with wagging tails and joyful leaps at the car, and she was forced to press down on her brake to keep from hitting them. The motor gave a tubercular cough and died, so she left the car where it stopped.

"Down, both of you," she begged, running across the grass

with them frisking around her. "Please, Switzy, I'm late."

The door opened just as she reached the steps and Peter stood there, wearing one of her frilly little aprons over his brown boxer shorts and holding out a glass. "Oh, darling," he mimicked, imitating her better than he thought he could, "I'm so relieved to see you!" Then he added in his own voice, "Where the dickens have you been?"

"At Midge's." Tippy took the glass and rubbed it across her forehead as he always did, though she was quite cool. "It's wonderful to come home to you, but turn-about's fair play," she said. "Were you lonesome?"

"Frightfully, but I haven't been here too long." He untied his apron and dropped it on a chair as they went into the living room.

Cool peace received them. Tippy made a great fuss of seating him in his chair, taking the lid from a box of cigarettes, seeing if the lighter worked, before she stood before him. "I have a lot to tell you," she said. "Would you rather have me sit in there beside you or recite it like a piece?"

"The chair holds two. I looked into that when we bought it."

He moved over ever so little and she crowded in with him, her flowered skirt spreading over his knees like a scattered bouquet. "It's kind of hard to begin," she said reluctantly.

"Is it about your doings of the day?"

"Partly, but it goes way back. It goes back, I think, to the day we came here." She tucked her shoulder under his and suggested, "Give me your hand to hold. I can tell it all better if I'm hanging on to you."

Their fingers met and interlaced so that their West Point rings were touching. Tippy traced around the twin sapphires with her other forefinger as she said slowly, "When we talked

WELCOME HOME, MRS. JORDON

about marriage, before we were married, we planned about quarreling. We decided just how we'd handle everything when we quarreled, but we didn't talk about what we'd do if we didn't pull together."

"No, we didn't. Haven't we pulled together, Tip?"

"I haven't. You pulled along just fine, but I kept things from you. I hated it down here. I was homesick and I hated it. And I told Penny about it instead of you."

Peter's heart skipped a beat. He thought of Penny's letter in the pocket of his shirt upstairs, of his own deception; and Tippy said into his silence, "Didn't you hear me, Peter? I said I wrote to Penny about it. I wasn't honest. I wrote her a private letter and I hid her answer."

"Yes, Tip, I know you did."

"You knew about it?" Tippy sat up and a flush spread over her face. "Did you read the letter in my desk?" she asked.

"I wouldn't do that, childie. Penny wrote to me. She told me you were homesick but not to worry about it. Being Tippy Parrish, she said, you'd get over it."

"I wonder why she told you that?"

"Because she knows I love you. Because even a blind man could see you weren't exactly happy."

"Oh." Tippy looked down at their rings, her wedding band uniting the two. "Oh," she said again. "Did Penny think there might be any other reason why I wasn't happy?"

"She didn't say."

"Did you?" Her amber eyes lifted to his in mute appeal, and it took all his courage to answer her.

"Yes, Tip," he said, "I thought there might be."

"You thought it was because of Ken." She didn't ask a question again, she answered her own. "Dear, foolish Peter and stupid Tippy," she said, her gaze steadfast. "There's only you.

Any other love I've ever had was small, compared to the love
I have for you. I can look back now and see why I never could
put you out of my mind and why I always turned to you when
I needed help or advice. Romance is one thing, Peter; and deep,
true love that's *mixed* with romance, and tenderness, and adora-
tion, is another. That's what I have for you. Please believe that."

"I do, childie. Now, I do."

"Just know. . . ." She took her hand from his and put both
arms around him. "Just know I've been foolish. I clung to
Mums and Dad—not Ken—just Mums and Dad and the family.
I couldn't bear to have their pictures out where they might
make me cry and you would see me, so I hid them. I hid them
from myself and I didn't tell you why. I let you worry. I was
pretty horrid, Peter."

"Is it over now?"

"It is if you'll forgive me. If you'll let me come close and be
a part of you again. If I can be a real wife instead of a spoiled
brat."

"What made my brattish wife wake up?"

"A lot of things. Penny's letter first. It made me mad. It
made me think I wasn't any earthly good until you explained
the difference between women and men one night. But I think
Gwenn did it, mostly. She showed me how wonderfully much
I have. The more she wailed the happier I got, the better I
liked my life."

"Good old Gwenn. She's worth the price of the telephone
call, isn't she?"

"And my new purple skirt." Tippy relaxed and leaned back
against him again. "She taught me one important thing," she
said.

"What's that?"

"To enjoy what I have. The girls, my life down here. You

know," she said softly, "I'm so happy I'm singing inside. I'm all over whatever it was I had, and I feel like looking at Mums and Dad again."

"Shall we bring them downstairs and invite them in?" he asked. "They'd like to see our house."

"From the knickknack table."

"And how about spending another eight bucks on a call of our own? How about telling them how happy we are?"

"Do you mean it?"

"I'll show you." He tried to get up with her in his arms, but she held him down.

"You're very sweet," she said, "but I like sitting in a chair with you better. And besides," she stated practically, "it's cheaper after six o'clock. Why hurry?"

Peter leaned back and looked down on the top of her bright head. "O.K.," he said. "But there is one thing I'd like to do right now, without having to wait for the time change."

"What's that?"

"You'll have to stand up. You'll even have to walk a little way."

"All right." She slid out and smoothed her skirt. "Now what?" she asked.

"We go outdoors." He led her through the hall with the two dogs trotting in front and expecting a romp; and he scolded good-naturedly, "Boys, get out of our way."

Rollo trotted out and down the steps but Switzy seated himself in the doorway like a front-row audience expecting to see a good show. "Why don't you go help Rollo find the guard?" Peter suggested. "Look. He's leaving you behind."

Switzy only wagged his tail in applause for a good first act, so he rolled his handkerchief into a ball and tossed it. "Fetch!" he ordered.

The little dog went bounding down the steps, and Peter turned to Tippy. "We've just arrived," he said to her puzzled smile. "Panama's our oyster and we're all set to open it up and find a pearl inside. Welcome home, my own, dear Mrs. Jordon." And he scooped her up and carried her over the sill.